999 B.C.

999 B.C.

Eye-Witness Accounts of the
Book of Jonah

Bob Larimer

To order additional copies of this book, contact:
Xlibris Corporation
1-888-795-4274
www.Xlibris.com
Orders@Xlibris.com
63522

DEDICATION

To Riki Kane Larimer, my wife and life support

PREFACE

This novella is based on the book I wrote for a musical play of the same name. To create songs for that musical I wrote lyrics for a dozen big-band jazz instrumentals that were popular in the '40's and 50's. Songs and Scenes from the musical, *999 B.C.*, are listed in the Appendix. You can listen to some of the songs at *SongsByBobLarimer. com.*

Characters and episodes in this story are freely adapted from historic sources. God's warning to Jonah that Nineveh would be destroyed, his survival in a perilous storm at sea, his claustrophobic three-day residence inside a giant fish and his recognition as a Hebrew prophet are all related in the Old Testament. Jeroboam was the name of several Hebrew kings of the Northern Kingdom, whose capital city was Samaria. The Philistines and Hebrews took turns conquering one another, the former ending up with the short end of the stick, their name serving as an epithet to this day. And archeologists credit the Assyrian King Tiglath with conquering most of what we now call the Middle East about three thousand years ago.

We know few details of events in those "pre-ancient" times. But this story was created on the presumption that the expression, "love makes the world go round" was as valid then as it is today.

1

PHILO

This is an age in which religious devotion is ascendant among the Hebrews, a radical shift I have been witness to during my long life. In the good old days, when I was in my prime, religious observance here in the Kingdom of Samaria was doubtless at its lowest ebb since Moses led his people out of the desert. It is the story of this dramatic turnaround that I will attempt to shed some light on as I put pen to scroll with an octogenarian hand in the year 949 B.C.

I should explain that the Hebrew prophets have long predicted something momentous will happen in the year, "Zero," which is why time runs backwards in this cockeyed kingdom. As to what it is that's coming, the prophets can't agree, and I could not care less. After all, I am a Philistine, a much-despised race in these parts, forbidden even to enter a temple of the Hebrews. They nicknamed me "Philo, the Philistine" at an early age as a constant reminder of my inferior station. They are loath to remember that we Philistines have a proud history in this region. Goliath, remember, was a Philistine and the greatest warrior of his time until David got lucky with a slingshot. That all happened before the Egyptians brought rack and ruin to our noble forbears, punishing them by driving thousands of Sidonians out of their homeland into ours. To this day Philistines continue to be bear the insults of maligners who equate us with those filthy, wretched Sidonians. But I digress.

The main events of this story happened fifty years ago in 999 B.C. I am prompted to tell my version by the recent release of the Book Of Jonah, a narrative that some respected scholars have dismissed as "beyond belief." It is surely one of the most amazing tales ever told: God selects an ordinary young man, Jonah, and says to him, "Forty days more and the city of Nineveh shall be destroyed. For its wickedness hath come before me." That was God's way of telling Jonah to get his ass to Nineveh and ask its citizens to repent. But instead of obeying the Lord, Jonah boarded a ship sailing across the Great Sea. Then God created a whale of a storm. (Excuse me, I'm getting ahead of myself.) God created a terrible storm, and Jonah was tossed into the sea. Now comes the whale. It says in this recently released Book Of Jonah that God rescued the poor boy by sending a giant fish to swallow him . . . if you can swallow that!

To know the real story, you had to be there. And I, Philo, the Philistine, was there. This very same Jonah worked for me as a scribe in the Royal Library fifty years ago when the saga began to unfold.

By law Philistines are forbidden to worship Yahweh, the god of the Hebrews. For they believe it was Yahweh who gave Samson the strength to bring the Philistine temple down on our heads after being betrayed by Delilah, a conniving Philistine seductress. This is pure poppycock, but the Hebrews were the eventual victors and so won the right to fabricate history. But I digress again.

We Philistines are at least permitted to idolatrize the Golden Calf, and I must say that holy cow has done well by me. By dint of hard work and a nose for politics, I rose to the most prominent position ever achieved by a Philistine in this domain—Lord High Keeper Of Scrolls And Tolls at the Royal Library of New Samaria, capital city of Samaria, the northern Hebrew Kingdom. In other words, I was Head Bookkeeper.

Business was booming in those days, especially at the Scroll Copycenter. Scribes labored day and night copying scriptures, royal decrees, letters for wealthy illiterates—not to mention wedding, birth and bar mitzvah announcements. All this had been made possible by the single dividend of an otherwise draconian Egyptian occupation: the introduction of papyrus. It has been a great boon to our libraries and a marked improvement over the clay tablets used heretofore. The Babylonians, in their usual arrogant and stubborn fashion, continue to etch cuneiform into weighty tablets that can and often do break the toes of their unfortunate scribes.

Also under my supervision at the Royal Library was the Bureau Of Divine Wisdom, a government monopoly on fortune-telling and headquarters of the Royal Prophetess, the Maiden Abigail. In theory there was only one Royal Prophetess. But prophecy was as popular with the public as profit was with the King. So we employed a large staff of Maiden Abigails. Some worked rotating shifts at the Library while others were out drumming up sales in the provinces.

At the Bureau of Divine Wisdom it was the duty of the Maiden Abigail to advise the King on vital matters, such as the best day to go into battle (which for him was never). She was responsible for royal weather forecasts and touchiest of all, the Queen's daily astrology reading. (Thank heaven nobody believes in that nonsense any more.)

The King had spared no expense in outfitting the Bureau with myriad tools of the prognostication trade—incense burners, amulets, scrolls of incantation, tarot tiles, a boiling cauldron. He saw no reason to limit the flimflam and flummery that could separate the citizenry from their shekels.

As assistant scribes, Jonah and his friend, Joel, pulled the holiday shift on the first morning of the new year, 999 B.C. And Abigail #42 reported for duty at the Bureau Of Divine Wisdom, where she donned the diaphanous robe of a vestal virgin and applied her seductive makeup. I remember her number well, because this Abigail was destined to play a key role in the Jonah tale.

Our growing business was cramped for space, so the Scroll Copycenter and Bureau Of Divine Wisdom were separated only by an improvised curtain that the randy young scribes could and often did peel back to flirt with the Maiden Abigails. But there was work to be done, so I patrolled the border between the two enterprises to discourage inter-office bantering.

It was customary on New Year's Day for the King and Queen to make a ceremonial visit to my domain. On the first day of 999 B.C. I was so busy reveling in my revelry I didn't so much as glance at a sun dial until nearly mid-day. After all, this had been a special new year. We had turned a momentous page in the calendar, from 1,000 to 999 B.C., calling for fervent and prolonged celebration.

As I belatedly approached the Royal Library I saw the monarchs' four-horse chariot parked in front, so I hastened to find an excuse for my tardiness. I dashed off to the house of a Philistine friend who boasts a spacious cellar of fine wines. There I procured a giant vessel of vintage wine sufficient to impress even the jaundiced eyes of the King and Queen. I would make my entrance with this impressive gift in tow, and hopefully, all would be forgiven.

2

JONAH

Certain dates stand out clearly in your memory as one ages while others fade away. The first day of the new year, 999 B.C., was one I remember vividly. It was shortly after my eighteenth birthday, my first New Year's Day at the Scroll Copycenter. I came to work with a buoyant heart. I knew that on this day it was customary for the royal family to pay their annual visit to the Bureau Of Divine Wisdom. The Bureau was separated from my workplace by an easily drawn curtain. So I felt certain I would catch a glimpse of the royal Princess Deborah—close-up and in the flesh.

I had been in love with the Princess for exactly 287 ½ days since the spring Passover Parade. My fellow scribe, Joel, and I were perched on a third-story window sill watching the royal family ride by in their golden chariots. The princess had been waving routinely to the cheering crowd when she noticed me on high applauding her fabled beauty. Suddenly her eyes locked with mine. Her outreached arms moved skyward as if to embrace me, and we shared a private moment of ecstasy that was unforgettable.

Joel tried his best to puncture my allusions. "It's the job of a princess to wave and smile at commoners in a parade," he said. "I'm sure she finds the whole thing a royal pain in the ass, especially the moronic likes of us on third-story window sills. She surely knows we're only up there to gape down at her cleavage." There was no way to convince Joel that Princess Deborah and I had shared a heart-stopping moment.

On New Year's morning I was so excited by the prospect of seeing her again, perhaps even locking eyes, that I carelessly spilled ink on my scroll. I was copying the first chapter of Exodus, and it would have to be redone.

Fortunately Philo wasn't around to witness my mistake and penalize me with overtime.

Taking advantage of Philo's absence that morning, Joel pulled back the curtain separating us from the Bureau Of Divine Wisdom and struck up a conversation with Abigail #42. He had confided in me he had a heavy crush on this particular Abigail. He thought 42 was a hot number.

"How's the weather looking tomorrow, Abigail?" he asked.

"Cool and cloudy with small slave-galley warnings," she replied. Then pulling back the curtain on her side, she spoke to me. "Wear your fur tunic when you go outside, Jonah. So you don't catch chilblains."

When Abigail returned to her divining, Joel said. "She has eyes for you, Jonah. Unfortunately she doesn't give a fig if I catch chilblains."

"I know how you feel about Abigail," I assured him. "I won't stand in your way. I remain faithful to my Princess Deborah."

"*Your* Princess Deborah indeed," he scoffed. "She doesn't know you exist."

We were interrupted by the unmistakable smell of steaming laurel leaves, which Abigail thrust toward me on a bronze tray.

"Jonah, I need your advice," she said. "The pattern of these laurel leaves foretell the Queen will gain weight this year—as much as ten cubic cubits."

"This will not endear you to her, Abigail." I ventured.

"I have an idea," said Joel. "You might say to the Queen: You will experience some changes. And they will weigh heavily upon you."

"That's perfect," Abigail agreed. "Thanks, Jonah." And she closed the curtain

"See what I mean?" Joel moaned. "She said, 'Thanks, Jonah.' It was my idea, so why not, 'Thanks, Joel?'"

"She probably meant to say, 'Thanks, Joel.'" I assured him.

"Thanks, Jonah." he replied.

Hearing brass fanfares and the roar of a crowd in the streets below, we rushed to the window. The King and Queen were stepping out of their chariot, but the object of my over-whelming desire was missing.

"The Princess isn't with them," I grieved. "Fate has defeated me." Joel hastened to close the curtain, as we scampered back to our desks. "Royalty impending," said Joel, "Look busy."

Shortly we heard the Queen's herald announcing her entrance: "Her Royal Highness, Azubah, Queen of Samaria," followed by her heavy, majestic footsteps.

We heard Abigail say, "Good day, Your Highness," a greeting we could assume was delivered in a prostrate position.

"You may rise, Prophetess," said the Queen. "Where is Philo, the Philistine? Why is he not here to greet his Queen?" She parted the inter-office curtain slightly and shouted, "Philo, darling! Where are you hiding, my little weasel?"

Abigail said, "I think he may be searching for his cat, Your Highness."

"More likely his catamite," replied Queen Azubah.

Then we heard the high-pitched voice of the eunuch, O'Badiah, who was the King's private herald and bodyguard: "His Royal Highness, Jeroboam, King of Samaria."

So there you are," said the Queen. "Poor Jeroboam. Always lagging behind."

"I was right behind, my sweet," said the King, then whispered to his eunuch, "And speaking of sweet behinds, who have we here?"

I knew at once that the King's roving eye had homed in on Abigail #42 and recalled what Philo once said of him: "Aside from his gluttony, vanity, sloth and cowardice, the King's principal weakness is women."

We heard Abigail greet the King and his solicitous reply: "I am flattered by your attention, my dear. And which Abigail might you be?"

"Abigail # 42, sire."

"Ahh, a recent acquisition. And a well structured one, I might add."

"For service to the Kingdom, your Highness."

"The King is often in need of servicing," he leered.

Abigail attempted to ward off the King's advances by turning tarot tiles. We could hear the crack of the tiles as the King continued his verbal assault.

"Dearest Abigail, do the tarot tiles foretell whether you will remain a maiden this year?"

Abigail slapped down another tile and announced her fortune. "Maiden!" she asserted.

"Still I am wont to open a channel of communication," replied the King.

"My channel is open only to astral spirits, Your Majesty." she answered.

"The King is wont," I joked to Joel, "but Abigail won't."

Enamored as he was of Abigail #42, Joel was not amused.

"That royal bastard—" he said. "rutting after a defenseless peasant girl. She's an orphan, you know."

Jeroboam's lecherous overtures were interrupted by a loud summons from the Queen: "Jeroboam!"

The King instructed O'Badiah: "Take note of the maiden's most extravagant wishes," then answered his wife dutifully: "Coming, my dear."

I peeked through the curtain and saw O'Badiah, with stylus and pocket scroll, trying to negotiate terms with Abigail #42, a familiar task for the King's eunuch. Abigail was having none of it, shaking her head, "No!"

Just then our boss, Philo, entered the Scroll Copycenter carrying an enormous vessel of wine. He was still dressed in the festive tunic and bejeweled sandals of his New Year's celebration.

"'Twas a riotous evening, my boys," he said. "And a raucous morning-after."

"The King and Queen await you," I told him pointing to the adjacent Bureau Of Divine Wisdom."

"Of course," said Philo. "Their royal butts await my loyal buss. What are their moods?"

"The Queen is strutting," I replied. "And the King is rutting," added Joel.

"All's normal then." said Philo. This monstrous vessel of wine should gratify even their greedy little hearts. Come now, carry it in for my audience." When Joel and I lifted the wine vessel to our shoulders, we realized the reputation of Philistines for great strength was more than justified.

Philo preceded us as we carried the enormous wine vessel into the Bureau of Divine Wisdom, where the Queen exulted, "Well, Philo, at long last!"

"My humblest apologies, most gracious monarchs," said Philo after much bowing and scraping. "I have been searching for a wine worthy of Your Majesties' quaffing."

"Ahh," said the Queen, admiring the huge wine vessel. "This is more than anyone can quaff. Except perhaps King Jeroboam."

Seizing the opportunity to flatter the King, Philo said, "Then in His Majesty's honor, let us henceforth call this giant wine vessel a 'jeroboam.'"

At a signal from Philo, Abigail No. 42 dipped two fine ceremonial goblets into the newly named jeroboam of wine and presented them to the King and Queen.

"May I propose a toast?" Philo asked.

"Yes, my loyal subject," said the Queen. "But only if you join us with your own goblet of wine."

Joel and I smiled to ourselves at the ease in which Philo had wormed his way back into the royal good graces despite committing the unforgivable sin of being late for a scheduled royal visit.

"To 999 B.C.," proclaimed Philo raising his wine goblet high. "To Your Royal Highnesses. To the great Kingdom of Samaria. And may interest rates remain stable."

3

PHILO

The Queen enjoyed her image of me as a libertine, and I had good reason to encourage that opinion. My good reason was O'Badiah, herald and bodyguard of King Jeroboam, and my secret soul mate. Love of a eunuch being a capital crime, our very lives depended on our discretion.

Intrigue at the royal court was thick and often lethal. My relationship with the Queen had provoked envy. Malicious lies were honed to a sharp point daily and aimed at my back. But I kept a step ahead of my enemies at court through a network of informants, among whom O'Badiah was best by far.

As the Phoenicians are fond of saying, "The camel does not see his own hump." Nor did my foes at the palace see me conspiring with O'Badiah.

His post kept him close to the King, who confided in him and sometimes asked for his advice. I was not surprised when Jonah told me he had overheard O'Badiah rendering pimp service to the King with Abigail #42. I sincerely hoped he would fail in that mission, because this Abigail was one of our top revenue producers. If she chose to surrender her virginity to the King, she would lose her credentials as a prophetess.

My precious eunuch, O'Badiah, was probably the most moral man I had ever known. Yet in the interest of serving our miserable King, he was forced to take on many disagreeable chores. He had long since learned, in the words of the Phoenician platitude, to "grin and bear it."

Despite its foul aspects, my beloved O'Badiah remained in the King's employ for my sake and in the interest of our continued forbidden affection. The notes he recorded by day I read at night. Thus did we outwit the formidable forces at the palace forever plotting to fuck the Philistine.

4

JONAH

Though I somehow stumbled into the profession of prophet and have been regarded as such for many decades, the truth is I was not a particularly religious person in my youth. Raised in the Hebrew faith, I had to memorize great swaths of biblical text, none of which stayed in my head for long. It seemed to me at the time that Abraham, Moses and other heroes of the Hebrew people lived in the distant past, and most of what they had to say was not relevant to modern times. I liked being a scribe, because it was a highly respected artistic craft. And although my work included copying lengthy scrolls of religious dogma, I was not required to believe a word.

So imagine my surprise on the morning when God spoke to me. Considering how it worked to my advantage, I sometimes wonder whether I conjured up the voice of God to suit my selfish ends. And yet hearing that voice, imagined or not, set in motion a series of events so implausible (well nigh impossible) they could hardly have happened without divine intervention. If one miracle is followed by another and another, is that not proof enough that God has intervened?

The first miracle was the appearance of Princess Deborah on a quay in New Samaria where I was fishing in the River Jordan. I had stopped there after work to take my mind off my disappointment when the princess failed to show up at the library on New Year's day. The quay was located in a tawdry part of town where immigrant Sidonian laborers stumbled out of mead joints and slept in the merchant stalls or passed out in the streets. It was growing dark and I was about to go home with my paltry catch when I saw a large chariot wheel being rolled in my direction. Behind the wheel, pushing and kicking it along, was a petulant young woman muttering under her breath. Seeing me, she stopped and said, with the sultry drawl of the southern kingdom, "Simple fisherman, could you oblige me with a drink from your goatskin bag?"

It was not until she had finished her question that I recognized her as the love of my life, Princess Deborah. I hastened to prostrate myself before her and apologize: "Sorry, Your Highness. Had I recognized you I would have groveled sooner."

"Please rise," said the Princess, pulling me to my feet with considerable strength. "I can't abide groveling. If only I could pass among my subjects incognito."

"Not so easy," I reminded her, "with your picture on every street corner."

"Oh, I wish Daddy-The-King wouldn't hang all those pictures of me," she said.

"Daddy-The-King must be very proud," I replied. "If a commoner may be so bold, you're even more beautiful than your pictures."

"I always say a commoner has as much right to admire me as anyone else," said the Princess. I marveled at her equalitarianism.

We were startled by the belch of a Sidonian sleeping on the quay. "Don't worry. It's only a drunken Sidonian," I assured her.

"They're all over town these days," she said. "Only yesterday I told Daddy-The-King he's letting in too many illegals."

I offered her my goatskin bag, and she seized it with gusto. "I wish I could offer water in a silver chalice," I ventured.

She hastily removed her fine chamois gloves, hoisted the bag and took a long, unladylike swig.

"Screw the silver chalice!" she shouted, "Bottoms up!"

After wiping her mouth on her sleeve, she let out a deep sigh of satisfaction.

"I forgot how good water tastes from a goatskin bag," she mused. "That's how I used to drink it before I was a princess. We were pathetic commoners just like you until Daddy worked his way up to King."

"Wow! I said, "How'd he do that?"

"Mommy poisoned his five brothers."

I hardly knew how to react and decided to be sympathetic. "Well, I guess they were really rotten uncles," I said

"Yes," she confirmed, "Gave me lousy Hanukkah presents. Even so, I made burnt offerings for them. Daddy-The-King says I shouldn't bother my pretty little head about such things. That's really patronizing, don't you think? Never mind. A fisherman wouldn't know what 'patronizing' means."

I thought it was time to introduce myself. "I'm not a fisherman. I'm a scribe over at the Royal Library. I'm Jonah Levine," I said with a cordial bow, "of the Literary Levines."

"And I'm Debby Cohen of the Royal Cohens," she replied, seemingly without condescension. Then she added, "It's such a pity you're not a fisherman."

Before I could ask why it was such a pity, she explained: "It's forbidden for a princess to mingle with the rabble. Compared with a scribe, it would be ever-so-much-more thrilling to mingle with a primitive, foul-smelling fisherman."

Of course any wish of the Princess was my command. "OK," I volunteered, "I'll pretend I'm a fisherman. And you can pretend I smell bad."

Accepting the invitation, she brought the sleeve of my tunic to her nose and gagged with delight. She was so convincing I had to check the tunic myself but could detect no bad odor. "Remember, you're only pretending," I said. Then, anxious to change the subject, I asked her about the big wheel she had rolled in.

"Came off my chariot," she said.

"Must have hit a pothole," I speculated.

"Yes," she agreed, "I must talk to Daddy-The-King about maintaining the infrastructure. My chariot was almost totaled. Habakkuk, my charioteer went to find a mechanic."

I shook my head: "A chariot mechanic? Good luck! You know what they charge for a tow job?"

"Outrageous," she said. "I blame the Guild of Chariot Artisans and Mechanics."

I couldn't resist showing off my knowledge of modern chariot technology by pointing out details of her wheel: "Class wheel here! Brass spokes, bronze hub, radial rim."

"If I didn't bring it with me, it would be stolen for sure," said the Princess

"Yes," I agreed. "This area is crawling with Sidonians. They've probably stripped your chariot by now."

Just then the sleeping Sidonian spoke a few drunken syllables: "Baktu veda habajalah."

"They refuse to learn our language," said the Princess. "And they take jobs away from native Samaritans."

"Samaritans won't do those menial jobs," I reminded her. "Like washing pottery and sweeping up camel dung."

"Maybe," she said. "But isn't it a nuisance the way Sidonians stop you on the road, wipe your camel's nose and look for 'baksheesh?'"

I had to pinch myself. Filthy fisherman or not, I was discussing political issues with the princess of the realm, who became more captivating by the minute. I tried to impress her by injecting a historical note.

"It's an old story," I told her. "King Solomon had his problems with the Canaanites."

"The Princess was about to discourse further on the subject of Solomon and the Canaanites when a chariot rolled up barely missing the head of the drunken Sidonian. O'Badiah, the eunuch who served as the King's herald and bodyguard, was driving.

"His Majesty, King Jeroboam of Samaria," announced O'Badiah.

The King leaped out of his chariot and rushed to embrace his daughter: "Thank God I've found you, my precious. The palace guards have been combing the city."

"My chariot broke down, Daddy-The-King," said Princess Deborah. "The charioteer went for help."

"And for leaving you unattended," King Jeroboam announced, "he is now beyond help."

"Poor Habakkuk!" replied the Princess. "I shall make a burnt offering for him."

The King abruptly turned his attention to me. "And who is *this*?" he demanded to know.

"Just a filthy fisherman I happened upon," said Deborah.

After such a dismissive introduction I felt I should explain myself to the King: "I'm not a fisherman, Your Majesty," I said with as gracious a bow as I could muster. "I'm a . . ."

"Jonah!" Deborah interrupted. She raised her finger to me as if reprimanding a disobedient child. ". . . filthy fisherman," I conceded.

Noticing that the Princess had removed her gloves, the King said, "Cover your hands, daughter. Have you no shame?" Then he turned menacingly to me: "It is unlawful for a commoner to behold the bare hand of a princess. And the penalty is death! Seize him, O'Badiah."

The eunuch throttled me in a powerful, vise-like grip before reminding the King: "I should advise him of his rights, sire."

"Oh, that folderol," said King Jeroboam impatiently. "Go ahead."

O'Badiah brought the blade of a sharp knife to my throat and said, "You have the right to be silenced."

"I waive my right," I managed to gasp.

The eunuch relaxed his grip, but held me firmly for interrogation by the King. "Have you seen the Princess's royal palms?" he asked.

I pretended not to understand the question: "What palms, Your Majesty? Does she grow royal palms?"

"You know very well what palms, you knave," the King growled. "The palms of her hands!"

At this point the Princess spoke up, but not in my defense as I had hoped: "You can't deny it, fisherman. I removed my gloves and you saw me stark naked—from my wrist all the way down to my fingertips. But you'll be dying for a good cause."

"What's that?" I asked.

"Me of course." she said. "I shall make a burnt offering for you."

The King patted his daughter's fair curls and spoke endearingly: "Don't bother your pretty little head, my pet."

The drunken Sidonian awoke briefly and slurred, "Pa-tron-iz-ing, pa-tron-iz-ing"—showing off a word he had just learned, and then dozing off again.

With my fate in his hands, O'Badiah said, "Your Majesty, if I may raise a point of law . . ."

"Yes," replied the King reluctantly, "But be brief with your brief."

"Under Samaritan law," O'Badiah pronounced, "it is obscene to view the royal palms of a princess with malice of forethought. But the Princess said *she* removed the gloves."

"And so?"

"So where is the malice of forethought, Your Highness?"

"Where is what?"

The Sidonian again dared to enter the conversation, parroting O'Badiah's words without understanding them: "Where . . . malice . . . forethought?"

Out of patience, the King put his hand on his sword but settled for a reprimand: "You stay out of this," he commanded.

It was then that my beloved Princess, in a reversal of roles, came to my rescue. She insisted that O'Badiah relax his death-grip, patted my head and pleaded for me as if I were a helpless animal: "I doubt the poor thing has much forethought of any kind. He was kind enough to give me water from his goatskin bag. Spare him, Daddy-The-King!"

Begrudgingly succumbing to his daughter's wish, the King instructed O'Badiah: "Free the prisoner."

Princess Deborah gave her father a grateful hug, and the King began marching to his chariot. "Come along, my dear," he said. Before the Princess could follow him, I ran to her and blurted out, "Debby, I must see you again."

Laughing at my presumption, she was quick to put me in my place: "Cool it, fisherman," she said. "You are so far beneath my purview it makes me dizzy to look down upon you. Besides, I am engaged to marry King Tiglath of Assyria."

Everyone in the Kingdom knew Princess Deborah had been promised to the King of Assyria. But it was presumed that because of his old age, nothing would come of it. "King Tiglath!" I remarked with disdain. "He's known to be a terrible tyrant."

"So's my mom," she replied, hastening to follow her father.

I kept pace with her and continued my argument: "Don't you know King Tiglath is so greedy for conquest they call him, 'Tiggy, the Piggy?'"

"Tiggy, the Piggy," she said. "Isn't that cute?" Then with a little wave: "Toodle-loo, my stinky fisherman."

Then suddenly she turned to me. For a moment I thought she was about to give me a farewell kiss. But no, she pressed her nose against my neck and said, "Just one more smell."

"So freaking bad!" she shuddered with delight as she leaped into the King's chariot.

The horses bounded away with the chariot and my Princess, leaving me in the solitary company of the drunken Sidonian.

"Go ahead," I called after her. "See if I care. Marry your cute tyrant!"

"Just my luck," I mused to myself. "I have to fall for a Jewish princess—the only one in the Known World."

If this is love, I thought, take it and shove it. If this is what the poets celebrate, let them choke on their words. If this is what the troubadours sing of, may they lose their perfect pitch. My frustration was so intense that despite a belief in God that was lukewarm at best, I made the mandatory bow in the direction of Jerusalem and addressed the Almighty by His holy name, a name that by tradition may be spoken aloud by Hebrews only within the sacred walls of a temple: "Yahweh, do you hear me? Can you ameliorate my misery?"

I received no answer from the darkening sky above, but the sleeping Sidonian below me on the ground spoke up: "I hear you, Jonah."

"I wasn't talking to you," I growled to the Sidonian, and he replied, "Funny, I could have sworn I heard you call my name."

"I called for 'Yahweh,'" I argued.

The Sidonian, who appeared to be talking in his sleep, said, "Yours truly," without the trace of an accent.

"I've heard of this phenomenon," I thought. "He's speaking in tongues. In my tongue."

As if able to read my mind, the sleeping drunk spoke again: "The Sidonian is not speaking. I am speaking, Jonah. Do you believe me?"

"I have to believe you," I replied. "No Sidonian can speak such fluent Hebrew. But I really was not prepared to hear the Lord speak through a drunken bum."

"I could speak through a rock or a bush, but that blows folks' minds," said The Almighty. "Now listen closely, Jonah. Forty days more and Nineveh shall be destroyed."

It was disappointing to hear Yahweh speak of a subject so far removed from what was on my mind. With little enthusiasm I answered: "Forty days more and Nineveh shall be destroyed. Got it, Yahweh!"

"For its wickedness hath come before me," the Sidonian's cultured voice continued. A long silence followed, and I feared Yahweh had left the premises. "Anything else, Mighty Yahweh?" I inquired.

"Just one more thing. What does 'ameliorate' mean?"

Before I could answer, the Sidonian awoke with a belch. Yahweh clearly no longer inhabited this poor sot, so I again bowed toward Jerusalem and raised my voice to the heavens.

"Now I get it, Yahweh," I said. "You have answered my prayers. The palace of King Tiglath is in Nineveh, and he is Debby's fiancé. If I hear Thou right, Yahweh, Thou are going to wipe out a hundred thousand people so I can marry the Princess. It seems like over-kill to me. I'd be happy if Thou just gave the old King a touch of the plague. But don't get me wrong. How Thou choose to assist me I leave entirely up to You—I mean 'Thou'—so long as the Princess will be mine!"

If this is love, I thought, it is the purest form of ecstasy. If this is what the poets celebrate, may they be rewarded on earth and in heaven. If this is what the troubadours sing of, may they sing with the voices of angels. Before long my beloved Princess will hear of the destruction of Nineveh and the demise of her fiancé. Then isn't her remembrance certain to turn to the adoring scribe she met on the quay? Or the filthy fisherman? I am all hers in whatever guise she prefers.

5

PHILO

The evening of New Year's Day O'Badiah reported that he had saved one of my scribes from execution. I was relieved. I couldn't afford to lose a scribe in the busy season.

The busy season had become even busier due to one of my better marketing ideas—condensed Bible stories. It had always seemed to me that the tales in the Hebrew Bible, while dramatic enough, were often bogged down with excess leaden prose that could easily be dispensed with. So I conceived the notion of a "Bible Readers' Digest"—released in installments, condensed but unexpurgated. Methodically I set out to remove the drivel from those ancient tales while leaving in the juicy parts. Unencumbered by stale accounts of ancient tribes and boring lists of who begat whom, my action-packed bible stories were an immediate popular success.

Freed of unnecessary distractions, the story of Joseph's rise to power after being sold into slavery by his brothers was gripping. Abraham's story of sleeping with the maid, supposedly for the sole purpose of birthing an heir, was titillating. And the story of Cain killing his own brother was morbidly fascinating. As for the Pharaoh's daughter, did she really find the baby Moses in the bull rushes or was this a cover-up? Readers of these scrolls couldn't resist my fast-moving tales of murder, seduction, sodomy and abduction—not to mention treason, treachery, incest and lechery.

My first order of business in the new year was to address the backlog of outstanding orders for my condensed bible stories. I would have to hire more scribes and extend the working hours of those currently employed. To impress the scribes with the urgency of the matter I showed them a sheave of orders received and already paid for: "Look at this," I told them. "Orders for seventeen more Genesis, nine Leviticus, thirty-two Exodus. How they love that parting of the Red Sea! Better get cracking, boys!"

Later that day the scribes had made excellent progress. In the late afternoon, when I allowed them a short break to massage their aching fingers, Jonah and Joel approached my desk. Joel spoke first. "Master Philo, you are a most learned man. May I ask you a theological question?"

"Yes," I replied, "but remember, I am a heathen."

"So you can be objective." was his answer. "Suppose God tells a mortal He plans to destroy the city of Nineveh. What would be His purpose?"

"Do you mean the Hebrew god?" I asked, careful not to speak His sacred name aloud. "And speaking to whom?"

"Yes, the Hebrew god speaking to Jonah," said Joel. "He spoke to him through a drunken Sidonian."

I was naturally incredulous and my reply took a sarcastic turn: "So a drunken Sidonian said God is going to destroy Nineveh?"

Jonah then spoke for himself: "Yes, in forty days. Believe me, sir, it wasn't the Sidonian speaking. It was the Almighty for sure. He said if He speaks through a rock or a bush, it blows folks' minds."

I could tell the boys were serious, so I thought it best to humor them. "Well, if it was your God," I said, "He is asking you to go to Nineveh and ask all sinners to repent."

"But why does He need me when He knows all and sees all?" asked Jonah.

I had recently read a treatise about this very conundrum by a notable Hebrew priest, so I was prepared: "When a teacher asks a question, does he know the answer? Of course. Your God, too, is always testing."

Jonah was not satisfied: "If God says Nineveh will be destroyed, it must be inevitable. Where do I come in?"

"According to your scriptures," I explained, "before God lays on a catastrophe, He often consults with a mortal, as with Noah before the flood."

"But why?" asked Joel, "Isn't He omnipotent?"

The question of how an omnipotent god can preside over an imperfect world has been wrestled with by better minds than mine. Nevertheless I felt obliged to come up with an answer: "It pleases your God to find a reason to be merciful. It pleases Him even more if Man, his creation, supplies the reason."

Our theological musings were interrupted by fanfares in the street below. Rushing to the window, I was surprised to see O'Badiah helping the King and Queen out of their chariot. Apparently they were making an unscheduled visit to my premises.

As I often do when trouble looms, I made light of it: "Speaking of God," I told the scribes, "Here comes a pair who think they outrank Him. It's my boss, the King. And his boss, the Queen."

I hurried to the Bureau Of Divine Wisdom to welcome my superiors. When O'Badiah failed to make his usual herald's announcement of the King's entrance, I knew this must be a matter of some urgency.

"Welcome, Your Majesties," I ventured. "And to what do we owe this enchanting surprise?"

"Cut the welcoming crap, Philo," snapped Queen Azubah. "We have serious business to discuss." Nodding in the direction of Abigail No. 42, she whispered: "In confidence."

Abigail got the message and exited the Bureau. "O'Badiah can stay," the Queen announced. "Eunuchs you can trust." Then, admiring O'Badiah's rippling muscles, she added, "Damn shame, isn't it? All that meat and no lentils."

We all enjoyed a moment of levity at the expense of O'Badiah, who threw me a pained look. But the Queen quickly got back to business.

"Let's get to the nitty-gritty," she growled. "Show Philo the message, Jeroboam."

Drawing an elaborate scroll from his tunic, the King said, "This just arrived by messenger from Nineveh. King Tiglath demands a matrimonial alliance with Samaria at once."

With this the Queen let out a cry of anguish: "No, no, never!"

"Well, we did promise Princess Deborah to Tiggy, the Piggy, Your Highness," I reminded her.

"Only because the old brute threatened war," she sobbed. "I refuse to deliver my precious daughter into the bloody hands of that monster, Tiglath. In that dreadful city of Nineveh."

King Jeroboam laid a comforting arm on the Queen's shoulder and attempted some solace: "Oh, Nineveh isn't all that bad. A lot of Samaritans take their kids over there to Nebuchadnezzar-Land, you know."

Through her sobs the Queen managed to give the King another order: "Tell him the rest," she whined.

"King Tiglath has dispatched an armada of ships to reach Joppa by the new moon," said Jeroboam. Opening the scroll, he scrutinized the manuscript with near-sighted eyes: "These are his exact words: You will deliver any and all Princesses for transport to Tarshish in Assyria."

"It appears he doesn't know we have only one daughter," said Queen Azubah sniffling into her royal handkerchief.

Warming to his task, King Jeroboam continued reading from the scroll: "Aforesaid Princesses must wear the veil of chastity and be chaperoned by the Queen Mother. The wedding will take place in Nineveh forty days hence."

"What else?" I inquired.

The King unrolled the scroll and said, "There's a note at the bottom. It says, 'P.S. If these demands are not met, it means war.'"

The Queen could no longer restrain herself and began to sob uncontrollably. Trying again to calm her down, the King displayed an engraved invitation: "But we're all invited to the wedding, my dear,"—which only made the Queen bawl all the louder.

"Tiglath's demands are unreasonable," I said. "To reach Joppa by the new moon, the Queen and Princess will have to leave on the morning caravan."

Suddenly the Queen stopped her hysterical sobbing and did what she always did best; she issued another command: "Call in the Prophetess, Philo. We're in dire need of divining."

I hastened to ring the gong summoning Abigail #42, who returned and began turning the tarot tiles. Despite the crisis of the moment, the King again turned his unwanted intentions on the maiden Abigail. "I'll consult the tarot tiles" he said and turning to Queen Azubah suggested, "Why don't you consult the boiling cauldron, my dear?" Then he turned to O'Badiah with a grin and whispered, "Jump in it perhaps."

Having much less confidence than the Queen in the art of divining, I asked O'Badiah to join me in the Copycenter. "While they consult the spirits," I suggested, "Let us consult our wits."

6

JOEL

I grew up on the same city block as Jonah, and we became fast friends even before we went to scribe's school together. Looking back to 999 B.C. fifty years later, I have to smile at my memory of the impressionable young Jonah. When he told me of his encounter with the Princess and his conversation with Yahweh, I thought he had gone off the deep end. Obviously his near-death experience at the hands of King Jeroboam caused him to hallucinate a dialog with the Supreme Being. And wishful thinking made him imagine that Yahweh declared He would destroy Nineveh.

Dubious as I was, I agreed that for Jonah's own piece of mind we would submit God's words for expert interpretation. We knew that our boss, Philo, was well schooled in Hebrew theology. He had studied the torah for years so he could advise the monarchs in their power struggles with the high priests of the kingdom. During the afternoon break, Jonah and I approached Philo and asked him to interpret God's words. Though he was as doubtful as myself that God had spoken to Jonah through a drunken Sidonian, he explained the meaning of the Lord's words (if they had indeed been spoken). In that case, Philo said, although God had not been explicit, his intent was clearly to send Jonah to Nineveh and ask all sinners to repent.

Before Jonah had a chance to contemplate a journey to the far-off capital of Assyria, we were suddenly interrupted. The King and Queen barged in on Philo bearing calamitous news. Their meeting took place in the Bureau Of Divine Wisdom, but Jonah and I overheard it all. King Tiglath had sent a message demanding that Princess Deborah be delivered to him at once for the purpose of marriage.

Jonah was distraught when we overheard that his beloved Princess would be on the morning caravan to Joppa, where she would board King Tiglath's ship for transport to Tarshish in Assyria. Without hesitation he vowed that he would be in that caravan and on that ship with his beloved. I think he intuited my intentions when he donned his outer tunic. How could I allow him to undertake such a dangerous mission alone? I could not.

"It's God's will!" Jonah exclaimed as we headed out of the Copycenter and pell-mell into an uncertain and dubious enterprise.

7

PHILO

As O'Badiah and I had anticipated, when we returned to the Bureau Of Divine Wisdom, the divining had yielded no actionable results.

"This thing is good for my sinuses," said Queen Azubah as she abandoned the boiling cauldron. "Aside from that, there is naught in the pot."

"Nothing in the tiles for Your Majesty," Abigail #42 advised the King, hoping to make her meaning doubly clear.

Meanwhile in consultation with O'Badiah, I had hatched a plan that I offered the Queen: "I have a thought, Your Highness, albeit fraught with peril."

With a nod the Queen dismissed Abigail #42 once again and when she was out of earshot, I continued: "Suppose we deliver a fake Princess Deborah. It would be dangerous because Tiglath may have agents in Samaria who might recognize the Princess."

Azubah turned her wrath on the King: "You have to hang all those pictures, Jeroboam!"

"Skilled cosmeticians can make most any girl resemble Princess Deborah," I told them. "The fake princess, however, must be a virgin who can pass the Assyrian chastity test."

"That's one test they can't study for," said a smirking Jeroboam, receiving a look that kills from the Queen for his trouble.

"But what about Princess Deborah?" asked the Queen.

"She will have to make herself scarce for awhile." I advised. "Later we can change her appearance and announce a new Princess. We might attribute her to one of the King's concubines."

"But the King has no concubines," said Azubah to Jeroboam with unaccustomed sweetness. "Have you, my dear?"

The King shook his head, with crossed fingers behind his back for my and O'Badiah's amusement.

"For this noble purpose," I said to the Queen, "You might permit him one . . . that is, if the King is agreeable."

"I'm certain he'd make the sacrifice," replied the Queen while Jeroboam smiled wanly.

My plan had improved the Queen's mood to such an extent that she impulsively embraced me. "If you can pull this off, my weasel," she said with a laugh, "I'll make you an honorary Hebrew."

"But where in this Kingdom are we to find a virgin?" queried King Jeroboam with a snicker.

"No doubt you've done your part to diminish the supply," Azubah admonished Jeroboam.

"I think it's doable," I assured them. "We can begin our search for a virgin among the Prophetesses—our Maiden Abigails, I mean. I can start by interviewing the Abigail now on duty."

"Number forty-two?" Jeroboam blurted out.

"How do *you* know?" asked the Queen.

"Just a lucky guess," replied the King.

I summoned Abigail #42 and much to her consternation, began fingering her hair. "It needs to be lightened," I said. "My colorist is a genius!"

"Dear Abigail #42, wouldn't you just adore being a queen?" asked Azubah solicitously. Abigail thought she was referring to me and was hopelessly confused.

"No, I mean a real queen," said Azubah, "Just like me."

"Just like her?" I overheard Jeroboam whisper to O'Badiah. "There has to be a better argument than that."

The King and Queen began to examine Abigail as though she were a prize steed. Looking in her mouth, Azubah exulted, "Good teeth! Deborah never had a cavity, you know."

Jeroboam tested the muscles in Abigail's upper arms. "Firm body," he observed. As his lecherous hand edged toward the girl's bosom, Azubah removed it and gave it a slap.

All this attention aroused Abigail's gravest thoughts. She was trembling as she pleaded: "Please help me, Philo." I asked Their Majesties' permission to take her aside. Then I explained the role we were asking her to play. If all went well, it would make her Queen of Assyria.

Unprepared as she was for this offer, Abigail requested some time alone to consider her decision. Her request was reluctantly granted, Queen Azubah reacting royally: "Doesn't anyone obey orders any more?"

"If her decision is favorable," I told them, "O'Badiah is licensed to conduct the examination for virginity."

Casting an envious eye on O'Badiah, the King muttered. "There are times when I wouldn't mind being a eunuch."

8

ABIGAIL #42

I have risen far from my peasant origins in my long life largely because of my mother. It was her tutelage that set me on the path to royal prophetess, an occupation aspired to by many and attained by few. Mom was reading tarot tiles to divine the futures of neighbors when I was a child. She later had a stall in the bazaar where she charged a shekel for her predictions. I learned from her how to impress fortune seekers with revelations that come as a surprise to them but are easily deduced from facts they have divulged themselves. She showed me how to read the stars in vagaries elusive enough to fit all outcomes. And she taught me tricks of the trade, such as how to make prophecies with magic beans—dried beans with living insects inside that jump mysteriously when warmed in the hand.

My mother also raised me with a keen appreciation of the importance of preserving my virginity. But it was my father, strong as Samson and skilled with spear and rapier, who kept the predatory boy-wolves at bay. Under his wary eye I survived puberty unscathed. When both my parents were swept away by the plague, I was sixteen and already enrolled in the National Divining Academy, well on my way to becoming a royal prophetess.

During my first few months at the Bureau Of Divine Wisdom, I spent my working days telling the fortunes of others without giving much thought to my own. Then on the morning after New Year's Day, 999 B.C., I found myself sitting alone in my dressing room pondering a life-changing decision, the nature of which I had become aware of only moments earlier. Suddenly the tables were turned, and I had to foresee my own future.

Though the vocation is respected and well remunerated with customer gratuities, a royal prophetess is trapped in a dead-end career. Because of the virginity requirement, she loses her job if she marries. Unable to meet eligible young men of her own class, she eventually resigns herself to spinsterhood.

That momentous morning, when Philo ushered me into an audience with the King and Queen of Samaria, I was at first perplexed and then frightened. They began critiquing my hair, my teeth and the condition of my muscles. I trembled because this was not unlike the examination that precedes being sold into slavery, a fate that befalls many Samaritans and is always to be feared. I asked myself what I could have possibly done to warrant the punishment of bondage. Had the King decided to make a slave of me so I would be powerless to resist his advances? Was Queen Azubah, having noticed the King's pursuit of me, in a jealous rage? With all his influence, was Philo unable to protect me? With these questions racing through my mind, I desperately whispered into his ear: "Please help me, Philo."

Detecting the fright in my voice, Philo took me aside and explained that I was a candidate for an important royal mission. When he explained its nature, I was both relieved and overwhelmed.

The decision I had to make could thrust me into the highest reaches of royal politics. It seems that years ago our King and Queen had agreed to a matrimonial alliance with King Tiglath of Assyria. Now Tiglath had demanded that the promise be made good by urgently delivering Princess Deborah to him for marriage.

Like other Samaritans, I had heard rumors that the King of Assyria was a monster whose excessive greed in conquest had earned him the nickname, "Tiggy, the Piggy." Given Tiglath's reputation, I wasn't surprised when Philo told me Queen Azubah was determined to thwart the tyrant's will.

I was quite surprised, however, when Philo asked me to be the means to that end. He said Princess Deborah and Queen Azubah would be leaving on the morning caravan to Joppa, thence by sea to Assyria. And how would I like to be the stand-in for the princess?

"Just imagine," Philo enticed me (as only Philo can entice)—"a lowly peasant girl from nowhere becoming queen of the Assyrian Empire, most powerful nation in the Known World."

At this point the lowly peasant girl's head was awhirl, and Queen Azubah was tapping her foot impatiently. She was not pleased when I said I needed some time alone to make my decision.

In my dressing room, I reflected on my lonely life in Samaria. My parents were gone. My affection for Jonah was hopelessly unrequited. On the other hand, as a queen I need never be alone. I would have slaves to do my bidding from dawn to dusk. In the royal court there might possibly be enlightened conversation and laughter, and I had had little of either lately.

Here my prospects of finding a suitable marriage would fade with my youth. As I grew older, it would become ever more difficult to play the role of seductive oracle my customers demanded. And the King's interest in me had put me in a most precarious position. On the other hand, in Assyria I could presume my position as queen would shield me from the attentions of licentious men. I would have to please King Tiglath of course, but in my profession I have learned to gently manipulate men of all ages, occupations and persuasions. I doubted that "Tiggy, The Piggy" would be an exception.

My thoughts then turned to Jonah. Joel had told me of his foolish belief that he would some day win the hand of Princess Deborah. I realized how devastated he would be by Deborah's marriage to Tiglath. But if I were to take the place of the Princess, he would at least have some meager hope.

I rang the gong to signal my readiness. When Philo appeared, I told him, "My answer is 'yes,'" and I began to undress. "So summon the eunuch," I said. "There is something he has to look into."

9

PHILO

After O'Badiah had verified the virginity of Abigail # 42, the Queen instructed King Jeroboam to escort Princess Deborah to the Priestess Hostel, where she would remain out of sight until after the wedding in Assyria. It was imperative that she not be seen by King Tiglath's many spies. After O'Badiah left with King Jeroboam, we worked almost until dawn transforming Abigail # 42 into a reasonable facsimile of Princess Deborah. Queen Azubah had put her entire boudoir staff at our disposal—a virtual army of skilled cosmeticians, beauticians, hair specialists, and experienced creators of royal robes, headdresses, veils and footwear. Working from portraits of the Princess, this talented crew turned Abigail into a Princess closely resembling the lovely Deborah and more than worthy of any king's desire.

The following morning the faux princess and I were driven by chariot to the Caravan Terminal and escorted into the magnificent tent that served as the terminal's Royal Class Lounge (monarchs and their entourages only). The tent, illuminated by oil lamps, was opulently furnished with giant feather-stuffed pillows for seating, urns filled with flowers, a table laden with food and wine. Queen Azubah had arrived before us and was pacing frantically.

I led Abigail to meet her and said with a bow, "May I present your daughter, the Princess, Your Highness?"

"Good work, Philo, said the Queen, "She looks like a princess all right. But it's doubtful she can act like one."

"When King Tiglath lifts her veil," I assured the Queen, "he will be totally captivated."

Abigail raised her veil. "My I remove it now?" she asked.

"Yes, but be careful," I warned. "Only the Queen and I are to know your identity."

"Have you brought your Certificate of Virginity, my dear?" the Queen inquired. Abigail produced a scroll which the Queen inspected. "Everything appears to be intact," she announced, then turned anxiously to me: "Philo, I'm so worried. I hear there are bandits and headhunters on the caravan trail. And cannibals!"

"No problem, just throw them a few Bedouins." I jested. "But I must ask you to come with me now, Your Majesty. The caravan is overbooked. We must use your royal clout to bump some commoners."

Outside the tent we heard a herald shouting, "Last call for passengers on Caravan 21 to Taanach, Megido, and all points north." The Queen look startled. "That's not our caravan, Your Highness," I told her. "Ours wends eastward to Joppa on the Great Sea."

10

ABIGAIL #42

I had never been paid so much attention in my life. "If this is what it's like to be a queen," I thought, "why did I even hesitate?" After hours of being pampered and fussed over—bathed, shampooed, oiled, powdered, measured and fitted with sumptuous garments—I was permitted a view of myself in the polished bronze mirror. I was so taken aback by my new visage that I looked behind me to see who was reflecting the image before me. Instead of the plain peasant, Abigail, I saw a veritable royal beauty, her hair golden as ripe wheat, her skin white as goat's milk. Breasts I had never been proud of had been molded by tantalizing décolletage to appear ravishing. Golden bracelets decorated my wrists dangling below the billowing sleeves of my sheared lambskin tunic. Gleaming silver anklets above my bejeweled sandals made the princess illusion complete. Only my fingers were invitingly bare awaiting the magnificent ring I could expect from my betrothed.

My transformation had an astonishing effect on me. I stood taller and prouder, brimming with confidence. I noticed that the staff who had transformed me were now treating me with greater respect. They knew I was not royalty, and yet my appearance drew an instinctive reaction of deference. Even Philo, accustomed as he was to ordering me around, seemed to humble himself when he said, "Your carriage awaits, Princess, to transport us to the caravan terminal." It made me smile to think that my boss, Philo, would be riding with me, yet he called it *my* carriage.

At the terminal Philo whisked me into Queen Azubah's presence in the Royal Lounge. I raised my veil, curtsied before her and spoke in the southern kingdom accent in which I had been so recently tutored: "I am your obedient daughter, Queen Mother, and shall try my best to be worthy of your trust."

The Queen admitted to Philo that I looked like a princess, then dismissively said she doubted I could act like one. Being a queen, it was impossible for her to even mildly entertain the notion that royalty had no monopoly on good manners.

Philo reminded Queen Azubah that her royal presence was needed to help him arrange first-class accommodations on the morning caravan. As they left the Royal Lounge, the Queen instructed me: "If you so much as smell a man, don the veil. Make sure no man gets even his camel's nose under your tent, my Princess."

Baffled by the Queen's command, I shrugged it off and sought to relax in the luxury of the Royal Lounge after an eventful and trying day. Surveying the opulence of the furnishings and abundance of food and drink in the Royal Lounge, I reflected on the privileges of monarchs that would henceforth be my entitlements. I had just settled into the soft comfort of a down-stuffed pillow when I was alarmed by the sound of muffled scratching at the far side of the tent.

"This is the Royal Lounge," I warned the intruder. "Entrance by commoners is forbidden."

The response was unmistakably the voice of Jonah: "Debby, my princess, is that you?"

I hurried to don my veil as an indistinct shape appeared at the tent's edge. Again imitating Deborah's southern kingdom accent, I asked, "Jonah, is that your camel's nose?"

"It's *my* nose," he said as his head and shoulders squeezed their way in. Then bouncing to his feet, he added, "and here's the rest of me."

I hardly recognized my dear Jonah in his shepherd's mantle with a hood that masked most of his face. "Why are you dressed like that?" I asked.

"Joel and I have joined the caravan as Bedouin guides," he replied, "so I can be near you and rescue you."

"You'd give your life for Princess Deborah, wouldn't you?" I marveled.

"Speaking of yourself in the third person is a quirk of royalty I'll have to get used to," said Jonah. "Why the veil, Debby?" and he tried to raise it.

I pulled the veil down firmly. "I can't show my face to any man, Jonah," I told him. "It's part of my bargain with King Tiglath." Then I damped down the oil lamps and lay back on one of the giant pillows. "I will take my veil off now, and you can kiss me in the dark. That way I'm still keeping my bargain with King Tiglath. Kiss me, Jonah."

I closed my eyes and waited for my beloved's first kiss. I had been puckered up expectantly for some time when I heard Jonah musing to himself. "This is truly amazing!" he murmured, "The Princess must be the most ethical person who ever lived. After all, nobody would ever know if she showed me her face."

I began to lose patience: "Where are you, Jonah?"

He continued to muse: "Yet because she made a vow, she must honor it, not withstanding . . ."

"So kiss me already!" I insisted. At last the kiss came. We locked lips and our bodies quivered as we lay entwined on the giant pillow. Our pulses raced, our hearts throbbed and we both moaned with the pleasure of our love—mine for him and his, not for me, but for the princess of my pretense.

Our kiss might very well have led to more serious expressions of desire. But before that could happen, we heard the fulsome voice of Queen Azubah outside the tent: "Princess! What's going on in there?" At the sound of the Queen's voice, Jonah beat a hasty retreat under the tent flap from whence he had come.

"I heard voices," said the Queen as she restored the light from the oil lamps. Thinking fast, I folded my hands and looked heavenward: "Just saying my prayers, Your Highness."

"That's commendable, my dear," said Queen Azubah, "A maiden's prayers are often answered."

"Sometimes in advance," I thought to myself. I slept blissfully that night dwelling on the sweet memory of Jonah's kiss.

11

PRINCESS DEBORAH

I was born a commoner and only became a princess when my parents usurped the monarchy of Samaria. I soon found that the lot of a princess is not as enviable as one might think. In fact when I relinquished my princess title mid-career, I didn't regret becoming a commoner again. As a princess, I was treated to every conceivable material luxury. But I was also denied the most important privilege in life—free will. From an early age my decisions were made for me, not by me. Stifled by this arrangement, I acquiesced until, in my eighteenth year, my parents plotted a deception intended to rob me of my royal birthright. Well meaning as they may have been, they had finally made a decision for me that was one decision too many.

I first got wind of the scheme afoot when I was visited by Daddy-The-King and the eunuch, O'Badiah, in my quarters at the palace. I had just told my new handmaiden, Hermes, my well kept childhood secret: When I was a little girl, I found that I could stand in one corner of my bedchamber and overhear everything the soldiers said in the palace armory on the other side of the wall. I called it my "listening corner."

"What you must have heard!" Hermes wondered.

"That's how I learned to cuss," I told her, and she exploded with laughter.

"Shh!" I whispered, because I had just heard voices coming from the palace armory. I led her into the listening corner.

"My daughter will not take kindly to getting out of town," we heard. I recognized the voice of Daddy-The-King. "We need a convincing plan or two."

"Plan A and Plan B." suggested O'Badiah.

"Exactly. Plan A is I lie and you swear to it."

"OK," replied O'Badiah. "What's Plan B?"

"You lie and I swear to it," my father answered. "Remember, it's OK to lie to a woman as long as it's for her own good. Let's go."

"But Your Majesty, what is the lie?" asked O'Badiah. "What exactly are we going to tell the Princess?"

"A routine lie won't do, will it? It will have to be a whopper," was the reply.

The two conspirators then lowered their voices so we were not able to hear the fiction they were constructing.

"You heard it," I said to Hermes, "Men only lie to us for our own good."

"They are so considerate, she replied. "What does one do when you know a man is lying?"

"Pretend to believe him of course," I told her. "So you can find out what he's hiding."

O'Badiah must have come up with a lie that tickled Daddy-The-King pink, because we heard him guffaw and exclaim, "That's a whopper, all right! Let's try it."

Shortly thereafter there was a knock on my bedchamber door. "Come in, Daddy-The-King.," I said.

"How did you know?" he asked as they entered.

"I recognized your knock," I explained.

Feigning the breathless anxiety of a bearer of bad news, my Daddy-The-King launched into a shameless prevarication: "My precious daughter, the Bureau of Divine Wisdom has notified me that a national calamity is imminent. The stars and planets predict a dreadful plague."

"What kind of plague, pray tell?" I implored.

"I can't bring myself to say." he groaned. "It's not fit for your tender ears."

I turned to O'Badiah for an answer, and he turned to Daddy-The-King for permission to speak.

Poor O'Badiah's high-pitched voice made his words seem all the more ludicrous: "I . . . er . . . uhh . . . they say it's going to . . . rain frogs."

Throwing my arms around Hermes, I put on a face of grief-stricken horror: "Oh, no! Not a rain of frogs!"

Showing greater acting talent than her station demanded, Hermes threw herself into the role of a thoroughly frightened handmaiden: "What are we to do?" she moaned and appeared to faint dead away on the bedchamber floor.

"We also bring news of your salvation, precious daughter," said Daddy-The-King. "The astrologers recommend the royal family go into seclusion for thirty days and pray for deliverance."

Giving a secret wink to Hermes, I replied: "We can be ready in a jiffy, Daddy-The-King. You just wait in the armory."

With great relief he said, "Well of course, my dear! When you're ready, my eunuch will escort you to a retreat of prayer at the Priestess Hostel."

As they left my bedchamber, the two could hardly hide their smiles, satisfied as they were with the ease of their deception. When the door had closed behind them, Hermes and I rolled on the bed with laughter. "What a whopper of a lie!" I said. Then we hurried to the listening corner, where I heard Daddy-The-King echo my sentiments to O'Badiah with delight: "What a whopper of a lie! I can't believe she fell for it."

"And I can't believe he thinks I fell for it," I whispered to Hermes.

"Now will we find out what they're hiding?" she asked.

I jumped up and down on the bed and shouted: "Will we ever!"

12

JONAH

When Joel and I impulsively dashed out of the Scroll Copycenter, I had no plan. I only knew that somehow we must join the caravan that would take my precious princess to the port of Joppa where she would board Tiglath's flagship. Arriving at the Caravan Terminal, we hid in the camel barn and overheard the drivers complaining about the heat, sandstorms and assorted miseries of the Joppa Trail.

"Worst of all," said one of the drivers, "is the smell of the filthy Bedouins we have to bring along."

"We need them though," said another. "When those desert brigands stop the caravan and demand bribes, they want payment in Bedouins."

"What do they do with them?" asked the first driver.

"I don't know," was the reply. "And I don't want to know. What I do know is for insurance we have to hire a few more before we leave in the morning."

As unattractive, even downright dangerous as it sounded, a plan had presented itself. Joel and I made our way to the nearest Bedouin enclave, where we found the residents more than willing to trade their bedraggled old hooded mantles for our splendid tunics. We returned to the camel barn in Bedouin garb and were promptly hired as baggage handlers (and bribes for bandits) on the caravan to Joppa.

That evening, we took cover outside the Royal Lounge tent, where we saw Queen Azubah arrive with her entourage, followed by Philo with the Princess Deborah. We overheard the Queen telling Philo that the caravan might be attacked by headhunters and cannibals.

"I have an idea," said Joel. "If we get a chance to talk with the Queen, we might be able to scare her so much she will refuse to go."

"It's worth a try," I said, "The Princess can't go without her. But queens don't talk with commoners, let alone Bedouins."

When we saw Philo leave with the Queen and her entourage, I realized Princess Deborah was alone in the tent.

"This is my chance," I told Joel. "I must enter and declare my love." Over Joel's objections, I found a loose corner of the tent and wriggled my way inside. As a man of honor, I will not describe Princess Deborah's greeting in detail but only say she gave me a kiss to remember. Unhappily, our memorable kiss was interrupted by the reappearance of Queen Azubah, and I barely escaped her notice as I scrambled from the tent.

I found Joel in our hiding place, and described my encounter with the Princess: "You have to believe me now," I told him. "She's nuts about me! She practically begged me to kiss her."

"Sure, sure," mocked Joel, "just like she opened her arms to you from her passing chariot."

I was moved by his skepticism to reveal more about the kiss than I had intended. "What a kiss!" I boasted, "It was, you know—what they call a 'wench kiss.'"

"A 'wench kiss?' With the tongue?" he asked incredulously.

"What more could a man ask for?" I said. "A princess—with experience."

From our hiding place we saw Queen Azubah pacing nervously around the perimeter of the Royal Lounge tent. If she would deign to speak with us, this was our chance to test our Bedouin disguises and accents. We put our heads together to come up with some off-putting stories that might make even this ballsy queen alter her travel plans. Then we stepped into the moonlight where the Queen would encounter us on her next trip around the tent. Much to our surprise, she spoke to us without hesitation: "Do you Bedouins speak the language of the Chosen People?"

"Poco, poco, Miss Majesty," Joel replied. "Poco, poco," I agreed.

"I must talk with someone, said the Queen. "I'm so worried about this journey I can't sleep."

"Don't have to worry" I assured her. "We be there."

"We keep eye on you," Joel added.

"Four eyes on you," I corrected.

"I've never been on the caravan trail to Joppa," said the Queen. "I presume you know it well."

Joel and I replied in exuberant unison: "Do we know the Yoppa Trail!"

"You mean the Joppa Trail!" she said.

"Si, the Yoppa Trail!" we shouted.

"I know it like back of my goat, Miss Majesty," said Joel, "Yoppa Trail mucho sandy."

"Yoppa Trail mucho dry," I added, clutching at my throat, "Dry make thirsty."

Joel faked a cough: "Sand make cough."

"All day long ride stinking camels," said Joel, demonstrating the discomfort of a camel ride: "Humpety-hump! Humpety-hump!"

"No water nowhere till come to oasis, Miss Majesty," I said.

Queen Azubah smiled with relief: "Ahh, an oasis. Tell me about it."

"We show. We tell. We show and tell," we recited together.

"Come to oasis on Yoppa Trail at dusk time," Joel explained. "Sing songs around campfire."

"How quaint!" replied the Queen.

"Campfires burn camel dung," I told her.

"Hot camel-dung smell bad," Joel said. "Roasted vulture smell badder."

"Make campfire under tree where dead bodies hang," I continued.

"What dead bodies?" asked the frightened Queen.

"Mucho evil men. They try to kill us," I replied.

"But we kill them instead," said Joel. "You don't have to worry."

"Oasis mucho romantic, Miss Majesty," I offered. "At twilight you hear wails of hyenas in heat."

"Si, mucho romantic," said Joel. "Scorpions do mating dance in moonlight."

Before we could lay the best part of our horror story on the Queen—how the cannibals seasoned and cooked the prey they kidnapped from the caravan—a breathless, frantic Philo appeared.

"Where have you been, Your Highness?" he asked. "The caravan is about to leave." He snapped his fingers in our direction: "Hop to it, Bedouins!" he commanded, "Fetch the Queen's baggage."

As we hurried to retrieve the royal luggage, we heard the Queen pleading with the Philistine: "I don't think I can go, Philo. I'm frozen with fear!"

"You have nothing to fear, Your Majesty," Philo told her. "Our brave Samaritan soldiers will protect you on the caravan trail. But if you don't show up in Joppa with a princess for King Tiglath, we don't have enough soldiers to stave off the raping, pillaging Assyrian hordes."

The Queen gasped at the mention of Assyrian hordes and started moving in the direction of the caravan to Joppa. Philo waved and shouted after the departing colossus: "I forgot to mention the good news. I managed to book you on a two-hump camel. Safe trip, Your Majesty!"

Then we overheard him mutter a parting comment to himself: "If you meet any cannibals . . . God help them!"

13

PHILO

After seeing the Queen and the newly created princess off to Joppa, I hurried back to New Samaria, where I joined King Jeroboam to hoist libations at his favorite mead joint. With the cat Queen away, the mouse King was in a mood to play. By the time I arrived, an excess of mead had already addled His Majesty.

Entering the mead joint, I heard him slurring his consonants as he spoke to O'Badiah, who stood guard at the door. "Look here, O'bee, my ball-less lad," he said pointing to the apron worn by a serving wench in attendance. "It says, 'Menorah Mead—The Brew That Slew Goliath!'" Noticing my entrance, he continued, "Good slogan, don't you think, Philo? I could use a good slogan myself." He pulled the startled serving wench into his lap and mused, "How about 'Jeroboam, the King whose thing is a fling with a wench?'"

Laughing uproariously, Jeroboam beckoned O'Badiah and me to join in his merriment. "I'll drink to that," I obliged. The serving wench refilled her pitcher from a giant urn of mead, and when she had poured drinks for us all, I offered a toast to the monarch: "Here's to the success of our pretender of a princess, Your Majesty."

"Yes, to Abigail Forty-Two," said Jeroboam. "One king's gain is another's loss. The Maiden Abigail stirred my heart immensely."

"And stirred you elsewhere perhaps," I suggested with a wink.

"True," the King admitted, "If only I could stop being a slave to my testicles."

"You can always lend your testicles to your eunuch," I said, much to the King's amusement and O'Badiah's embarrassment, "He will return them in good condition—used, but in good condition."

"But why pine for Abigail when I can pluck this pretty posy?" asked the King as he bounced the serving wench on his lap. The bounce gave the poor girl her chance to escape his drunken clutches. She ran giggling from the room with Jeroboam in hot pursuit.

"That's the true sport of kings, O'Badiah . . ." I jested, ". . . wench-chasing."

Far from being placated, O'Badiah was seething with resentment. "You can always lend your testicles to your eunuch!" he said. "How can you demean me so, Philo?"

"Sorry, my dear," I told him. "But it's my duty to entertain the King. And the King likes eunuch jokes."

"Everybody does," he replied. "I am sick and tired of eunuch jokes." Then mocking the type of jokester he abhors, he mimicked, "Whatta you stuff in your codpiece, big boy—pomegranates?"

The serving wench ran back into the room, circled our table and ran out again with a panting, inebriated King Jeroboam running doggedly behind.

Hoping to improve O'Badiah's foul mood, I tried to distract him by describing the chase as a chariot race: "It's Serving Wench in the lead, Jeroboam coming up on the outside."

But O'Badiah remained coldly silent. "Your skin is much too thin" I told him. "You should let the jokes slide off."

"And you should enlarge your repertoire," he countered. "Don't you know any vestal virgin jokes?"

The serving wench reappeared, circling the table with Jeroboam hanging on to her apron strings. "Looks like they're coming into the stretch," I said.

The King took possession of the giggling wench once again and fondling her on his lap, asked me, "Did you see the Queen's face when you said I'd have to take a concubine?"

"Priceless!" I answered, "But why just one concubine, Your Majesty? You like your ladies petite. So take two, they're small."

My levity had the desired effect on the King, but after an appreciative guffaw, as often happens with the intoxicated, his mood suddenly turned dark. He released the wench with a pat on her fanny and turned to me somberly. "I'm uneasy, Philo." he said. "If King Tiglath gets wise to this plot of yours, he'll march in and hang all of us up by our balls."

Seeking to restore the King's festive mood, I replied, "Well at least O'Badiah doesn't have to worry about that." My remark so offended my beloved that he pointedly turned his back on me.

"Can you never be serious, Philo?" said Jeroboam. "Until Abigail Number Forty-Two is safely married to Tiglath, how can we sleep at night?"

"We can't possibly," I agreed. "So . . . we will dance the nights away! My sovereign, I have a brilliant idea. Since we have to be in Nineveh for the wedding anyway, why don't we just haul our jolly butts to that fun-filled city posthaste and soak up some local color while we're unencumbered?"

The King got my drift: "Without Her Ladyship, you mean?"

"Yes, Your Majesty," I replied, "A little release from the awesome travail of being top dog. We'll find the best shell games in Nineveh." Then trying to soothe O'Badiah, I turned to him and added, "I hear they have special games for eunuchs."

"I just thought of something funny," said the King, "The Queen is sailing to Tarshish. And she gets deathly seasick."

"That clinches it then!" I replied and dancing jauntily around the table, I exercised a talent I am known for at the Royal Court: I improvised a bit of catchy doggerel:

> *"While the Queen throws up in the deep blue sea,*
> *The King lives it up in Nineveh—with me."*

I had not personally experienced the delights of that wicked city, but I had heard many a lurid tale of its provenance. My sources informed me that Nineveh caters to every vice ever heard of, plus many novel and inspired inventions. Comparatively, Samaria was an uptight, bridled, restricted society where God's commandments were not always adhered to but were at least taken seriously.

When I described my hearsay of nude dancing girls and orgies in the public baths in Nineveh, Jeroboam raised his mead vessel in jovial endorsement.

"Nineveh is lower than Sodom," I told the King, "more vile than Gomorrah." He cackled with joy.

"And you know what God did to Sodom and Gomorrah," O'Badiah muttered to me. "Nineveh's turn is coming."

"Don't be a spoil sport," I whispered. But I was taken aback by his comment. O'Badiah had not heard Jonah's story about God's intention to destroy Nineveh. Yet through his own unswerving righteousness, he had come to the same conclusion.

My reflections were suddenly interrupted by a commotion behind the giant urn of mead. While filling her pitcher, the serving wench had seen someone hiding in the urn's shadow and cried out. Reacting quickly, O'Badiah dragged a slender hooded figure from behind the urn. He locked the interloper's neck in a powerful grip and shoved the suspect before the King. "Your Majesty, this is doubtless one of King Tiglath's spies," he said, "and disguised as a temple priest."

The altercation had frightened and sobered the King. He complimented O'Badiah: "Good work. He must be dealt with."

Pulling a knife from his tunic, O'badiah would have made short work of the purported spy had I not intervened. "Hold on," I shouted, "Shouldn't we question him first?"

The King agreed: "Yes, unmask him."

O'Badiah pulled his prisoner's hood down, and we were astonished to see that it was none other than Princess Deborah. Choking from Obadiah's stranglehold, she staggered dizzily into the arms of her father. "My poor darling daughter!" he said and turned sternly on O'Badiah: "You nearly killed her!"

"Are you alright, my angel?" he asked the princess, "Is anything broken?"

"Physically, I'm OK," she replied weakly. Then regaining her strength with surprising alacrity, Princess Deborah thrust her fist forcefully in the King's face and launched a vengeful verbal assault: "But I am extremely pissed off at you, Daddy-The-King! I only pretended to believe your lies so I could find you out. Raining frogs, indeed!" Imitating her father's instructions, she mocked him: "The royal family must go into seclusion for thirty days and pray for deliverance." Still in a rage, she pushed the King's vessel of mead under his nose and asked, "Is this how you pray for deliverance?" Then she shoved the hapless serving wench toward her father and demanded to know: "Is this your holy priestess? And who dreamed up this dirty scheme to rob me of my birthright?"

It was now my turn to be the butt of her wrath: "I'm sure it was you, Philo! And another thing—who the Hell is Abigail Number Forty-Two?"

Bowing to the princess, I tried to maintain my composure. "Am I to understand, Your Highness," I asked, "that it is your desire to become Queen Of Assyria?"

"Your damn-tootin' it is," she answered. "How long can I wait for Mister Right-King to come along? My royal career track in Samaria is a dead-end. I could be stuck here at the Princess level for life."

"We were only trying to protect you from the brute Tiglath," I assured her.

"Is he a man or not?" she asked, "Puts his sandals on one at a time?" When I conceded both points with a nod, she snapped, "Then I can handle him!"

The King intervened: "But darling, your mother said . . ."

Interrupting her father disdainfully, Deborah wanted to know, "Do you have to do everything Mother tells you, Daddy-The-King? Don't you have a mind of your own?"

"Of course I do," replied Jeroboam.

"Then do what I say for a change," said the Princess. "Send a message to King Tiglath. Tell him you made a mistake. You sent the wrong daughter."

"What kind of mistake?" the King asked.

"Tell him you're far-sighted," she suggested.

"He'd never believe . . ."

"Tell him the truth then." retorted the Princess. "The Queen is bringing an imposter."

"You can't do that, Your Highness," I said, "The Queen would be executed."

The King seemed to be contemplating this outcome favorably, but Princess Deborah was in no mood for further discussion: "Philo, I order you to commandeer an express caravan to Nineveh." Turning to the King she added, "As for you, Daddy-O, I'm putting you in custody of the high priests for your own safety until Mom gets back."

Grasping Jeroboam's ear, the Princess led him to his fate as she mused to herself, "Which suits me best I wonder—'Queen Deborah of Assyria' or 'Deborah, Queen of Assyria?'"

"Incredible, isn't it," the King said to me admiringly as he was led off, "how much she resembles her mother?"

I weighed the consequences of Princess Deborah's decision with my beloved: "This is the greatest quandary of my career, O'badiah. If I obey the Princess, I disobey the queen and vice versa. Either way I'm a goner."

"You did it again, Philo." he complained, "You told the King another eunuch joke."

"This is no time to quarrel, my swain," I replied, "You can see I'm at my wit's end right now—juggling our affairs, keeping all the balls in the air."

"There you go again, said O'Badiah, "You said, 'balls.'"

"You may be sick and tired of eunuch jokes," I replied, "Well, I'm sick and tired of having to watch every word I say. You're driving me nuts."

"You said, 'nuts,'" O'Badiah moaned, with tears now misting his eyes.

I could tell he thought this was a kiss-and-make-up moment, but I was much too exasperated to play that game. "Go ahead and pout if you must," I said. "I have to go now and order a caravan as the Princess directed."

As I made my way to the door, the serving wench sidled up to O'Badiah and took hold of his codpiece.

"Whatta you stuff it with, big boy?" she asked merrily "Partridge eggs?"

14

JOEL

The camel drivers worked Jonah and myself hard on the desert trail to Joppa. Upon arrival at the port, they rewarded our labor with enough shekels to buy seafarer's garb to replace our Bedouin robes.

In the port of Joppa Tiglath's flagship had arrived from Assyria and was dockside awaiting provisions for the return journey. We watched as Queen Azubah and Princess Deborah, in royal robes and veils, were escorted aboard. We presented ourselves to the harbormaster, who hired us as stevedores to carry supplies up the gangway. Once aboard, we made the acquaintance of Captain Hiram, a bearded old Phoenician seafarer who commanded the ship. We told him we were experienced sailors ready to join his crew. As soon as he looked at our hands, he knew we were lying, But as luck would have it, a couple of his sailors had jumped ship. So Captain Hiram reluctantly recruited us as deckhands.

After three days at sea we hadn't seen hide nor hair of Queen nor Princess. The scuttlebutt on board was that Princess Deborah had been nursing a seasick Queen.

"When we get to Tarshish," Jonah said, "they'll relax their guard on Princess Deborah, and we'll make our move."

"What about your duty to God?" I asked. "You're supposed to be warning the people of Nineveh."

"God can wait," Jonah replied. "He has eons of time."

"Here that, Lord?" I said, speaking facetiously to the heavens. "Patience!"

We were manning the steering bar at the stern of the ship. It was a calm, sunny morning on The Great Sea, and I was in an expansive mood. Born in a

Samaritan coastal town, I had hung around ships as a boy and knew something about them. "Working this ship's a pleasure," I told Jonah, as I admired the grain of the cedar steering bar. "It's the latest Phoenician Sport Galley. The power train features a VX mizzen sail. Real powerhouse below deck too. Thirty Babylonian musclemen supercharged with Egyptian slave drivers smoking papyrus."

"Sounds like this baby is virtually storm-proof," said Jonah hopefully.

Captain Hiram appeared starboard pointing to the fiery horizon: "Red sun in the morning, sailors' warning," he announced ominously, "There's a big blow coming, me boys!"

"Aye, aye, Captain Hiram," we chimed in. And as if triggered by the captain's prediction, the sea became choppy and the ship began to rock. Great storm clouds seemed to appear out of nowhere. Rain began to pour, soaking us to the skin, accompanied by claps of thunder and bolts of lightning.

"Attention all hands," shouted Hiram, "Steady as you go. The storm has announced its arrival!"

"They say this ship is virtually storm-proof, Captain," Jonah ventured.

"Yes," he answered. "And if we sink, we'll only virtually drown." Then he rushed to the speaking tube used to communicate with the slave drivers of the oarsmen below deck. "Now hear this, slave drivers," he announced. "Power up to quarter-fast. Give the oarsmen a double ration of mead."

From the speaking tube we heard the voice of the slave driver-in-chief: "Aye, aye, Captain Hiram." Just then a great wave pounded the ship knocking us all to the deck. As we struggled to regain our footing, Captain Hiram shouted joyously over the wind and waves. He was, as the Phoenician saying goes, "in his element."

"Hey, that was a sock-a-roo!" he yelled. "It's getting really interesting now. Right, boys?"

Frightened out of our wits as we were, we tried to show our commander we shared his courage. "Right you are, Captain," we exclaimed.

Our shouts were drowned out by three enormous, ear-splitting bursts of thunder. Both Jonah and I had the distinct impression that it was the voice of Yahweh. For the thunder claps seemed to clearly pronounce the three syllables of "Nin-e-veh,"

"Did you hear that?" Jonah asked. "God commands me to go to Nineveh."

Suddenly his legs took on a life of their own and propelled him mindlessly to the ship's railing. Only my arms locked around his waist prevented his jumping overboard.

"We're far out to sea," I shouted. You could never swim to shore."

"If I stay onboard, everyone will die," he replied, "including my beloved Princess."

Again the thunder seemed to unmistakably speak the three syllables of the Assyrian city: "Nin-e-veh!"

"If God is speaking, He's only reminding you of your duty," I told him as I pulled him off the rail.

"Back to the steering bar, boys," shouted the captain. "I need more muscle here."

We joined him and three giant and hairy crewmen in the nigh impossible task of holding the foundering ship on a windward course. With a crash, the mid-ship mast fell to the deck and was blown into the sea, which appeared to delight Captain Hiram: "We've got a missing mizzen mast!" he crowed with a hearty laugh.

Then we saw Queen Azubah and Princess Deborah inching their way toward us, holding tight to the ship's railing. Despite the gale-force winds, somehow their royal gowns and veils stayed respectfully in place.

15

ABIGAIL # 42

It had been an arduous journey, but at long last the camel caravan brought Queen Azubah and myself safely to Joppa. With the aid of spirits and balm, which it was my duty to administer, she weathered her fear of cannibals and the discomforts of the desert with a queenly demeanor. We grew closer on the journey. In fact she told me more than once I showed her greater consideration than did her daughter.

Jonah had finagled his way onto the caravan posing as a Bedouin guide, with no knowledge of the desert whatsoever. And Joel, a loyal friend indeed, had joined Jonah's mission to rescue the Princess, not knowing of course that she was me.

I had many opportunities to make my identity known to Jonah—on the evening of our kiss in the Royal Lounge tent, on the caravan to Joppa and later aboard King Tiglath's flagship. I can hardly explain why I continued the masquerade. Deep down I must have enjoyed Jonah's pursuit of me even though it was not actually me he was pursuing. I could have easily ended the whole charade but instead chose to prolong it.

On board the ship in the Great Sea my seasickness wore off on the second day, but the Queen's misery continued. Weakened by her inability to keep food down, she insisted I stay in her cabin at her beck and call. From our cabin window I could see Jonah and Joel working on deck. I often saw Jonah surveying the Queen's cabin looking for his beloved princess. But I stayed out of sight, and Her Majesty's presence kept him at bay.

A storm began on the morning of the fourth day at sea and grew with terrifying force. The only saving grace was that the Queen's fear of the storm's fury soon abated her sea sickness. Late in the day several crewmen came to our cabin, which stood alone near the ship's helm and bore the full force of the mounting waves and wind. They had orders from the Captain to move us to safer quarters near the stern.

We departed the cabin in the nick of time. For as we inched our way sternward, hanging on to the ship's railing and our crewmen saviors, one of the ship's masts crashed down on what had been our cabin. Both mast and cabin were swept into the sea. Arriving at the ship's stern, we saw that Jonah and Joel, with other crewmen, were manning the steering bar, desperately trying to hold the ship on course as Captain Hiram shouted orders to the slave drivers below deck.

The Captain greeted us with more panache than the circumstances seemed to call for: "Greetings, monarchs," he shouted over the wind, "Been a most entertaining day, don't you think?"

"Our cabin has blown into the sea," said the Queen, "and we almost went with it—if that's what you call entertainment."

"Something to relate to your grandchildren," answered the Captain cheerfully.

Jonah left the steering bar and seized the chance to speak with me, his supposed beloved: "This is a wonderful storm, Princess Deborah," he said.

"Hardly wonderful if it drowns us," I replied in my best southern kingdom accent.

"Wonderful because it brings us together," he said. "I have memorized your beautiful face, which appears so often in my dreams. It's as if I can see right through your veil. I love you, Debby. Tell me you love me too."

I obliged him truthfully with the three little words he wished for.

When Jonah heard them, he raised his fist to the heavens and shouted, "How about that, Yahweh? She loves me!"

Three ear-shattering claps of thunder were the heavens' response. With the ship pitching and yawing dangerously, Captain Hiram rushed again to the speaking tube: "Now hear this, slave drivers. I declare a *red* emergency. Row for our lives." To underscore his point he began singing lustily: *"Row, row, row the boat."* From the speaking tube came a chorus of oarsmen chanting their reply: *"Row, row, row the boat."*

"Is there anything I can do to help, Captain?" volunteered Queen Azubah.

"I humbly request that you join me in prayer, Your Majesty," Hiram answered.

"But what god should we pray to?" pondered the Queen.

"We better try them all," suggested the Captain.

I reflected that as a seaman Captain Hiram must have rubbed shoulders with crewmen and passengers of every faith, belief, creed and superstition in the Known World. Confirming my thoughts, he launched into a wide-ranging prayer to assorted gods he had heard appealed to by frightened voyagers in his long career at sea. He offered ardent prayers to the fierce African gods of thunder and lightning, the gods of Egypt (Horus, Iris and Bast), the ancient Babylonian god, Baal, the Assyrian goddess, Asura—even the devil down under.

Irritated because Captain Hiram had failed to beseech the Hebrew god, Queen Azubah issued a challenge on high: "Yahweh, I am the Queen of the Hebrews. Are we or are we not your favorite race?"

The Queen's plea was greeted by the most terrifying burst of thunder and blast of lightning we had yet experienced. It was enough to convince Captain Hiram that if we were to survive, Yahweh was indeed the god he would have to make a deal with.

"Someone on this ship is doubtless the cause of your anger, great God of the Hebrews," he shouted to the heavens. "You have only to point him out to me and I will have him thrown overboard."

Jonah abruptly fell to his knees before the Captain: "I am the cause of it all!" he confessed. Then he rose and jumped onto an emergency rowboat hanging on the port side. "I have put love above my duty, Yahweh. I beg you to spare the innocents on board." Standing in the little boat, he was ready to jump into the sea.

I ran to him crying, "No, no, Jonah," threw myself into the rowboat and grasped his sailor's shirt to restrain him. He leaned over to give me one last kiss through my veil, which, soaking wet with salty seawater, could not have been all that satisfying.

"And especially spare my beloved princess," he implored the heavens, then leaped into the tempestuous waves, leaving me holding a fragment of his torn shirt.

I was certain my love was a goner now. Yet I shouted hopelessly into the unforgiving wind: "Jonah, you've made an awful mistake! You died for the wrong girl—me, Abigail." Speaking to the heavens, I issued a final appraisal to the Almighty: "You might call it an ironic tragedy, God. He unwittingly died for a girl he didn't even like that much."

To my amazement, in the short time my account to God had taken, the vicious wind turned into a tender sea breeze, the raging waves were becalmed and the sun shone blissfully on our storm-battered ship. Celebrating the miracle, Captain Hiram offered a grateful prayer: "We thank you for ending the squall, great God of the Hebrews. And for accepting the sacrifice of the poor young deckhand who is now lost in the briny deep. He must have pissed you off immensely, because on his behalf you scourged us with the most malicious storm ever encountered by a highly accredited and well credentialed Phoenician sailor man—namely me."

While the ship's crew and passengers gave thanks to our God, I remained in the emergency rowboat, sobbing with a deeply felt guilt. Jonah's demise was obviously and entirely my fault. An honest word from me and he would have headed back to Samaria and Princess Deborah. I didn't fully understand why I had played this nefarious game with such catastrophic consequences. The most generous answer was I wanted Jonah to be near me, the least generous that I was consumed by jealousy of Princess Deborah.

Looking seaward in my reveries, I realized that the suddenly calm seas meant Jonah might possibly be afloat and alive. I released the towlines of the rowboat and fell with it into the sea. I would rescue my darling Jonah or die trying.

16

JONAH

Through a series of subterfuges and lucky breaks, Joel and I were able to stay on the trail of Princess Deborah across the desert to Joppa and onto King Tiglath's flagship. I had just about concluded that my conversation with Yahweh on the quay was, as Joel diagnosed it, an illusion brought on by romantic wishful thinking. But with or without Yahweh's assistance, I was determined to follow my precious Debby and win her hand, forbidden palm and all.

On the fourth day at sea a storm struck with such fury that it unsteadied even our ship's stalwart Captain Hiram. When we heard thunderclaps that clearly spoke the word "Nin-e-veh," Joel and I realized that Yahweh did not take lightly my failure to go directly to that wicked city. The storm was clearly an expression of Almighty anger. But frightening as it was, it did have the desirable effect of chasing my beloved Princess out of her cabin and into my arms. With the storm raging, I was able to speak with her and declare my love. Though she remained veiled, when she said, "I love you, Jonah," in her lilting southern-kingdom accent, she was unmistakably Princess Deborah, and I was enthralled. Unfortunately I then rubbed it in with the great Yahweh—shouting to the heavens, "Hear that, Yahweh? She loves me!" Not to be trifled with, He immediately raised the storm to a level that would soon send us to the bottom of the sea.

When Captain Hiram began to pray, I knew it was time for me to come clean. I confessed to all aboard that I was the cause of the storm. Then I jumped over the ship's railing and landed in the emergency rowboat lashed to the port side. As I was preparing to leap into the sea, my brave, beloved princess was suddenly at my side attempting to restrain me from suicide.

Before throwing myself into the deep, I gave her a farewell kiss through her water-soaked veil. It was a salty mouthful. But I remained mindful that she was veiled because she was honoring her vow, an impressively ethical stance on her part in the midst of a raging storm. And that was my last thought as I fell into the Great Sea.

17

JONAH

I must have lost consciousness when I hit the water, because the next thing I remember was waking up in what appeared to be a dark and forbidding cave. But I soon sensed that the cave was moving, and the sound of heavy breathing confirmed the worst: I was trapped inside a living beast. My prison was a monstrous cavern of membrane with walls of giant vertebrae alternating with seams of blubber. What I recognized from anatomy studies as a huge epiglottis dangled in the beast's throat. I had heard and seen drawings of the giant fish known as a whale but never actually seen one, let alone been inside one.

The floor (I don't know what else to call it) inside the whale was littered with detritus of the sea that had been randomly swallowed—ships' timbers, driftwood, palm fronds, seaweed, fruit that must have floated from the shore and an abundance of fish, some so fresh they were still flopping. The shaft of light above was streaming from an aperture, which I recalled from my anatomy lessons was known as the creature's "blowhole."

The whale's heartbeat could be heard and its reverberations felt as the great beast plowed through the waters. When I tried to stand, I found it difficult to keep my balance. I stumbled and fell, then paused to consider my dire circumstances. I was thankful to be alive, of course, but my situation was altogether perilous and terrifying.

I wanted Yahweh to know my feelings. But to speak to Him I first had to ascertain the direction of Jerusalem, a difficult task in the belly of a moving whale. I took an educated guess and bowing in that direction, I said, "Wow, Yahweh, I must have really pissed you off! If you are testing my wits, you win." I continued at length in that vein but receiving no response, I decided to make the best of a bad deal.

As minutes turned to hours and hours turned to days, I was able to survive on fruit and fish. Fortune had smiled by providing a swallowed knife, so I dined on peaches, apricots and slices of raw fish. From the timbers I fashioned a dining table, a chair and a makeshift bed with a mattress of palm fronds. I had no way to keep track of time, but the light from the blowhole separated night from day. When it was clear that I had resided in this bizarre mobile home for nearly three days and nights, I again vented my wrath to the heavens.

"Where are you, Yahweh?" I cried. "You don't speak to me. You don't send a message in a bottle. Be reasonable, Lord. You've made me suffer enough. You've had your fun."

As if in response the whale suffered an attack of the hiccups. Envision a human hiccup, multiply it a thousand fold and that will give you only the faintest idea of the force of a whale hiccup. Each occurrence sent me flying precariously through the air along with my makeshift furniture and the assorted debris I had so laboriously arranged inside the whale.

Thinking I had nothing to lose, I was now in the mood to actually threaten the Lord. "Now you've gone too far, Yahweh, I warned. "I swear, if I ever get out of here I'll write my own book of the bible and tell the world what you really are: A cold-hearted bully! A diabolic SOB! A sadistic old fruitcake!"

My tirade was interrupted by the sudden arrival of another swallow-ee. Caroming down the whale's throat in the emergency rowboat, where I had last seen her, came the Royal Princess Deborah. Or so I thought.

I raced to greet my beloved: "Debby, my darling!"

Then I knelt humbly to thank the Lord I had so recently excoriated: "You've answered my prayers, Yahweh. Never mind the names I called you. You're a just dude after all."

Having hopefully squared things with Yahweh, I hastened to help my princess out of the boat. "Hold onto my arm, my angel," I told her. "It'll be difficult at first to keep your balance, but you'll get the hang of it. And you can uncover your face now. You know the old song . . ." My joy knowing no bounds, I serenaded my beloved with an improvised ditty:

> *"No one wears a veil*
> *In the belly of a whale."*

She offered no resistance as I swept her veil away with a flourish. I was shocked to find that the face I had unveiled was not that of my princess. It was the different but all-too-familiar face of Abigail # 42. I'm ashamed to say the only greeting I could manage for the Royal Prophetess was a curt, "Oh, it's you." I callously withdrew my helping hand and she fell indecorously back into the boat.

It was time for me once again to berate Yahweh: "Hey, you really know how to jerk a guy around. You blindsided me into thinking this poor provincial kid from the office was my beautiful Princess!"

"Jonah," said Abigail, "it's really rude to carry on a conversation without introducing the third party."

Seeing that the poor girl was still struggling to get out of the rowboat, I minded my manners and lent her a helping hand. I attempted to explain my on-again-off-again relationship with the Almighty: "Yahweh's not actually here, Abigail. I'm just pointlessly venting my wrath." Then I continued to pointlessly vent: "As I was saying, that was a sick joke you played on me. And why involve Abigail #42 in my punishment? The least you could do is let me perish in peace."

"You mean we're doomed in here?" asked Abigail.

"There's very little data on survival rates inside a whale," I told her. Not even much anecdotal evidence." Then I picked up a fish and added, "But pretty soon we'll run out of sushi."

"There's flint and tinder in the rowboat," she said cheerily. "We can cook the fish."

"I like mine pan-grilled with frankincense and myrrh," I jested and then inquired: "How did you of all people end up here dressed up in Princess gear?"

"Well, I of all people was recruited as a lady-in-waiting to the Princess," Abigail replied. "In the court of King Tiglath, of all places."

"So you were on the ship with the Princess," I said.

"Yes. And when you jumped overboard, the Princess ordered me to rescue you."

"She ordered you to risk your life for me? She loves me that much?"

"Yes, she confided her deep feelings for you."

I felt my heart jump for joy: "Hurry. Tell me exactly what she said."

"She told me about your passionate kiss at the Caravan Terminal," Abigail replied. "She is tragically torn between her love for you and her duty to the Kingdom. I would go so far as to say the Princess worships you, Jonah."

I attempted a celebratory cartwheel but the whale's motion made for an awkward landing. I shouted insolently to the absent Yahweh: "You're not the only who gets to be worshipped," Then it occurred to me how futile was celebration in the present predicament: "Ahh, what's the use? Yahweh isn't listening."

Abigail had picked up a water-sculpted piece of driftwood and was carrying it to the opposite side of the whale's interior. "We should try to make the best of it, don't you think?" she said. "This driftwood would look better over here."

"Just moved in and already redecorating," I observed.

"We should really hang curtains on that ugly skylight," she said, pointing to the blowhole above.

"That's the blowhole where the whale breathes," I explained. "We'll die soon enough!"

Calm and brave as she had been, Abigail was unsettled by my realism. She had tears in her eyes as she approached with her arms outstretched. "If we have to die," she sobbed, "let us be in each other's arms."

I resisted her entreaty, but she persisted: "You can pretend I'm the Princess if you like," she said. "And I'll imagine you're the man I love."

"I didn't know you were in love," I said as I backed away.

"Yes, madly," she replied. "I'll pretend you're him, and you can pretend I'm the Princess. We'll pretend to get romantic."

"Some place to get romantic!" I observed as I surveyed our surroundings.

"Come on, kiss me," she implored, doing her sultry Royal Prophetess best.

"No, not in the belly of a whale," I demurred.

"One little kiss, what does it matter?" she pleaded.

"The ambience does matter," I insisted. "And you can't know my feelings. You're love can't be as all-consuming as mine."

"Now you're condescending," she replied turning away. Then she reached out to me again: "Can you at least hold my hand? I think that's moonlight spilling in from the blowhole."

"Sure, that old devil blowhole," I quipped.

My sarcasm was rewarded by a sudden jarring movement of the whale that knocked us both off our feet. "Feels like the whale's taking a dive. If so, we'll soon run out of air."

Abigail rolled toward me and clutched me in a desperate embrace. Realizing there was no longer any hope of claiming Princess Deborah, I felt obliged to honor Abigail's last wishes. Even more persuasive was the effect of Abigail's soft body squirming invitingly against mine. "OK," I said, "Go ahead. Try to convince me I'm kissing the Princess."

Our lips met. But the motion of the whale had become so spasmodic it was a struggle to complete a full-blown kiss. When our lips unlocked, Abigail registered a blissful smile.

I spoke first: "I hope you were able to pretend I am the one you love."

"Yes," she said. "I have a good imagination."

"I tried to imagine you were the Princess." I admitted. "But I'm afraid kissing you isn't the same."

"It's true what they say about love," said Abigail. "It's all in the mind."

I heard her remark without comprehension, because the whale's movement had taken a new direction, heading for the surface at breakneck speed. I rushed to the rowboat and retrieved enough flint and tinder to strike a fire, which I quickly brought to bear on a pile of dry driftwood.

"I'm lighting the driftwood," I told a frightened Abigail. "Our last hope is that the smoke will choke the whale. He may cough us up—if we don't suffocate first. Hurry get in the boat with me."

Abigail was quick to accept the invitation. "Oh, Jonah," she said, clambering into the boat and plopping directly on top of my prone self. "Hold me close. I don't want to die a virgin, do you?"

It was a question I never thought I would have to ponder. "No," I admitted. "I guess if there's anything worse than dying young, it's dying a young virgin."

"So hurry," said Abigail. "Whatever it is, do it. Do you know how to begin?"

"I think so," I replied meekly. "But we don't have much time for foreplay."

The smoke was thickening as our inexperienced hands explored one another and fuelled our desire. Our stumbling efforts were decisively interrupted and our mutual virginity preserved. For the smoke suddenly took its intended effect on the whale, and its gigantic cough catapulted our little boat up and out of the beast's throat with a mighty thrust. Abigail and I were locked in a tight embrace as we prayed for a safe landing.

18

PHILO

As I had told O'Badiah, Princess Deborah's order to arrange an express caravan to Nineveh put me in a perilous position. The fastest land route to Nineveh would take us through hostile territory populated by tribes of murderous bandits. It was my hope that we could survive this first leg of our journey and get to Nineveh before the Queen and her fake princess, who were taking the longer, safer route by sea to Tarshish, thence overland to the Assyrian capital. If we won the race to Nineveh, Deborah's introduction to King Tiglath would be made before the Queen arrived. Deborah's legitimate claim to be Queen of Assyria would dramatically shift power in the region from mother to daughter.

The instinct for survival that had kept me alive and well throughout my career had always been guided by a single precept: follow the power. So, for better or worse, my allegiance had now been swiftly transferred to Princess Deborah. I executed her commands with my usual speed and efficiency, which soon earned me her praise and confidence.

Our caravan wended its way northwest to the Great Sea. We arrived on the shore after a week of relentless sandstorms, miserable to endure yet fortuitous in keeping the bandits in their caves. We set up camp on an accommodating beach, watered our camels and looked forward to following a safe, well traveled trail northward to Nineveh.

The caravan cooks had just rung the dinner bell when the surf swept a small wooden rowboat onto the beach. Princess Deborah and I approached it gingerly to see whether there was anyone aboard. We were amazed to find my scribe, Jonah, and Abigail # 42 entwined in the bottom of the boat.

We were stunned into silence, but Deborah finally spoke up: "Well, if it isn't my filthy fisherman locked in conjugal embrace with what appears to be an ordinary slut."

Jonah leaped from the boat to correct the Princess's impression: "Debby, my love, you know I'm not a fisherman."

"And that's no ordinary slut," I said. "That's Abigail Number Forty-Two."

Deborah pointed to the disheveled girl in the boat and asked me: "Is this the Abigail Mommy has been palming off as 'moi'? This frowsy floozy?"

Abigail was miffed and spoke to the Princess in a manner she would never have dared before becoming faux royalty. "You try spending the night in the belly of a whale," she said, "and see what it does for your hairdo!"

The whole conspiracy began to dawn on Jonah. "When you said, 'palming off' did you mean Abigail Number Forty-Two has been posing as . . . as . . . you?" he asked the Princess.

"You have my royal assent on that," replied Princess Deborah.

Jonah turned to Abigail: "So it was you I followed . . . and kissed in the tent, not the Princess."

"I'm afraid so, Jonah," Abigail admitted.

"Boy, have I been hoodwinked!" Jonah said, his temper rising. "You even made up all that stuff about how much the Princess loves me, didn't you?"

Abigail was moved to tears. "I wanted you to die happy," she sobbed.

Jonah beseeched the Princess. "I followed Abigail because I love you, Debby," he said. "I thought she was you. How foolish of me to think that she could possibly be the beautiful, unmistakably regal you."

I sought to spare Jonah further embarrassment: "The Princess intends to marry King Tiglath. We journey to the wedding by Express Caravan."

"Don't take it personally, Jonah," said Deborah to my scribe. "Marrying a king is just more my speed."

"But I risked my life for you," Jonah replied, "disobeyed God for you!"

The Princess was dubious: "Disobeyed God? You gotta be kidding."

"Jonah believes Yahweh ordered him on a mission to Nineveh," I told her.

"He did!" Jonah added. "But I disobeyed him for the sake of the Princess. So He caused a whale to swallow me."

"How can you say you're not a fisherman," Deborah asked him, "with a fish story like that?"

"It's true about the whale, Princess." confirmed Abigail. "I know because I was in there with him."

"Well, there goes your reputation," said Deborah. Then turning to me, she asked: "Philo, you don't believe this nonsense, do you?"

"I'm skeptical of course," I answered. "But Jonah has somehow come to shore precisely where we stopped to encamp with our caravan. That's either dumb luck or an act of God."

Deborah shrugged: "I say dumb luck."

O'Badiah, who had been respectfully silent up to this point, ventured an opinion: "If it was an act of god, then Jonah is obviously a . . ."

We all knew the sacred word he was about to utter. Filled with awe, we spoke it with him in unison: ". . . prophet!"

"Would that be a major or minor prophet?" asked Princess Deborah.

"Can you believe that bitch?" Abigail whispered to me. "She's trying to decide if a prophet is a better catch than a king."

"All our interests converge in Nineveh," I told her and Jonah. "So join our caravan. We depart at dawn."

With renewed interest in Jonah, Deborah agreed: "Yes, come along, Jonah. I can use an additional footman."

"Foot man?" said Jonah. "I'm more of a leg man myself. But whatever turns you on."

19

JOEL

I had joined Jonah's mission to follow and rescue the Princess because he was a dear friend and I feared for his safety. But I never shared his belief that his love for Princess Deborah was reciprocated. I appeared to be wrong when I saw the Princess lower a rowboat from our storm-rocked ship in a desperate attempt to save Jonah after he leaped into the sea. She did indeed love Jonah, I thought, and was even willing to die for him.

When King Tiglath's flagship arrived in Tarshish, I was in a quandary. Should I return home to Samaria or suffer the long trek over the mountains to Nineveh, where I might fulfill Jonah's mission for him posthumously? I decided on the more adventurous course, and when I reached Nineveh, I found Jonah was there ahead of me—as if risen from the dead. He was already making a troubled name for himself in the Assyrian capital. Dressed in dirty sackcloth, his face smeared with ashes, he carried a placard on a stick that said, "THE END IS NEAR—9 DAYS LEFT."

We had a joyful reunion. Had I not known Jonah as the epitome of honesty I would have doubted his amazing tale of the whale that swallowed him and Abigail—and their rendezvous with Philo and Princess Deborah. It was not the Princess who had followed him into the Great Sea, I now discovered, but Abigail #42. Her dedication to Jonah had not altered his love for the Princess. But the whale episode had convinced him his first order of business in Nineveh was to obey Yahweh.

I was quick to follow Jonah's example, adopting sackcloth and ashes as my dress code and carrying my own placard with my own succinct message: "REPENT OR DIE!" As we ardently sought acolytes in Nineveh's bawdy red-light district, we passed dozens of hole-in-the-wall joints advertising

Nude Dancers, Peep Shows, Orgy In Progress and the like. Hawkers stalked the side paths drumming up business. Curious to find out what was on offer, I asked one what could be found inside.

"Hot infotainment!" he said.

"What kind of infotainment?" I asked.

"Pedophilia, phallophilia, necrophilia," he replied. "What's it to ya?"

"It's three of the reasons God will destroy Nineveh," said Jonah. "That's what's it to us."

Taking notice of our doomsday signs, the hawker invited us in: "So check it out before we all check out."

Amidst the raw temptations surrounding us, we raised our dissenting voices: "People of Nineveh, mend your ways! Mend your ways or God will end your days!"

"That's catchy," said Jonah. "Keep it in the pitch."

"How about this?" I suggested. "Read God's lips—apocalypse."

We were beginning to have some fun with our doomsday mission, creating original, clever admonishments.

20

JONAH

I was happy to be reunited with Joel and to have a companion in my growing unpopularity as I spread the bad news in Nineveh. On the day he joined me we outwore our welcome in the red-light district and were roughly escorted out of the neighborhood. Undeterred, we continued to declaim our warnings in a better part of town, where our dire predictions were greeted with tolerant smiles and outright laughter by the worldly, upper-class residents.

As luck would have it, we ran into Queen Azubah and Princess Deborah as they stepped out of a swanky boutique. Philo and O'Badiah were carrying their numerous, weighty purchases.

"What's this?" the Queen asked pointing in our direction. "Extremely unseemly, these religious fanatics." Philo recognized us at once and tried to mollify the Queen. "So they're Samaritans," she declared shrilly. "That's even worse. Stirring up trouble in a foreign country."

"What god do you presume to serve with this balderdash?" she asked me.

"Almighty Yahweh, Your Highness," I replied.

"For the wickedness of Nineveh hath come before him," Joel explained.

"Give Yahweh a break, boys," said the Queen with an air of despair. "He can't keep up with the sins of Samaria, let alone Nineveh."

I dared to raise an important theological question: "Do you think Yahweh is interested only in Hebrews, Your Majesty?"

"Yes, and even that seems to be fading," said Queen Azubah glumly and signaled her entourage to follow her to a waiting chariot. When the Princess lingered, I rushed to speak with her.

"I guess you're still hell-bent on marrying Tiggy, the Piggy," I said, and when she nodded, I added: "You never even had a date with him." Referring to my "End Is Near" sign, I concluded: "At least with me, you get a known quantity."

"You mean a prophet of doom," she replied dismissively. "I've been looking into it, Jonah. And most prophets have lousy marriages."

"Well, God does send us on the road a lot," I admitted. "But I . . ."

"Who's that?" Deborah interrupted pointing to my fellow scribe.

"That's Joel. He's a friend at the office."

The Princess made no mistake of her attraction as she sidled up to Joel.

"They must call you, 'Joltin' Joel,'" she purred, and when Joel shook his head, she said, "You sure are jolting me, pretty boy! What brings you to Nineveh?"

Pointing to his doomsday sign, Joel explained: "I'm kind of like helping Jonah out with his project."

"And why did you smear those silly ashes on your face?" she cooed, stroking his cheek: "I know. So the girls can't see you're handsome as Samson."

"The ashes are a symbol of atonement," said Joel.

"What are you atoning for, honey?" Deborah asked. "We haven't done anything yet. How long will you be in town, Joltin' Joe?"

Consulting the latest number on my sign, he replied, "Just a few more days."

The designs of my Princess on Joel sent my spirits plummeting. How could she try to seduce my friend in my presence after I had endured so much for her sake? I was on the verge of despising her when she suddenly turned away from Joel, threw her arms around me and whispered: "I was flirting with your friend just to tease you, my filthy fisherman." Then she gave me a quick peck on my lips, not a real kiss but enough to make everything I had suffered for her heretofore more than worth it.

"Mumsy awaits me," she said as she bade me farewell and ran off to join her mother, the Queen.

21

PHILO

My goal was to bring Princess Deborah to King Tiglath's palace before Queen Azubah arrived, and we succeeded. But it was a hollow victory. When we arrived at the palace, we were told that the King had taken his army on maneuvers. The next available appointment for visiting royalty would be two days hence.

When Queen Azubah arrived on the following day, I was prepared to be severely chastised for aiding and abetting her daughter's betrothal to the brute, King Tiglath. But the Queen was lenient with me. She understood I had no choice but to follow the commands of her strong-willed daughter. And she was grateful that I had brought her dear Deborah safely to Nineveh. As usual, she pinned all the blame on King Jeroboam, whom she assailed as too weak to hold the Princess safely at home in Samaria.

But the Queen was far from content with the thought of her daughter in the hands of an old, rapacious tyrant. She had conceived a plan to save Deborah from the fate the ambitious princess was so diligently seeking. Before I realized it, Azubah's plan had become my plan. And once again, my Philistine ass was on the line.

22

PRINCESS DEBORAH

It was exhilarating to be in charge of my own future for a change. As soon as we arrived in Nineveh, Philo escorted me to the palace where I presumed my marriage to King Tiglath would be promptly signed, sealed and delivered. Alas, the king was off with his army, which delayed our betrothal. I was disappointed but at the same time encouraged by the news. For if the monarch was in the field leading an army, he was certainly not a dilapidated old weakling In fact I was excited at the thought of my fiancé on the battlefield in shining armor and couldn't wait to make his acquaintance.

My mother, the Queen, and Philo arrived on separate caravans the next day.

It was a tearful reunion that soon led to a serious argument about the wisdom of my determination to be Queen of Assyria.

"I'm marrying King Tiglath," I told them. "Period, end of sentence."

"Yes, and it could be a life sentence," said my mom with a maternal sigh.

"Such a headstrong child!" she complained to Philo. "She refuses to hear your plan."

"We have a plan, Princess," said Philo with his usual insinuating charm. "Please do us the courtesy of listening. I simply suggest that the Queen present two daughters to King Tiglath—you and Abigail. Then . . ."

"That cheap bimbo?" I interrupted. "No way!"

"But it's entirely for your benefit," said Philo. "It greatly improves our bargaining position when we negotiate the prenuptial agreement."

"In case of divorce you get the palace," said my mother.

"The King will much prefer your royal bearing, of course," Philo told me. "But two princesses will give us leverage. We can make him pay."

I found the very thought of Abigail being considered my equal, even as a negotiating ploy, nauseating to the extreme. "It demeans me greatly," I told Philo, "to present the King with a lowly, unmannered peasant wench as if she were authentic royalty such as myself."

"Abigail Number Forty-Two is nothing but a bargaining chip," he assured me. "She will be used only to your advantage."

I remained suspicious. "No funny business?" I asked.

"Only money business," said Philo.

As the only legitimate Hebrew princess, I felt on solid ground and reluctantly agreed to the proposition. "You will be held accountable though," I warned Philo.

"Of course," said Philo. "But understand. I will not be present when you and Abigail are presented to the King tomorrow. Only royalty are permitted."

Mumsy was distressed: "I can't bargain with the King without you, Philo," she whined.

"If only I could be a Philo on the wall," he said.

"Not on the wall!" she insisted. "I want you beside me in King Tiglath's throne room. That's an order."

"I hear you, Your Majesty, said Philo. "But some orders are impossible to . . ." Before he could finish O'Badiah whispered in his ear, and he corrected himself: "Some orders must be followed, so something might be improvised. If you will excuse us, Your Highnesses."

Philo and O'Badiah had no sooner made their hurried exit when my mother said, "We must rehearse our audience with King Tiglath, my dear. I will summon the other princess."

"Please don't refer to that little tramp as a princess except when absolutely necessary, Mumsy," I replied. "Remember what Philo said: She's nothing but a bargaining chip!"

23

PHILO

When I advised Queen Azubah that I would not be permitted to be in their royal company for the audience with King Tiglath, she insisted she could not bargain with the King without me. I saw no answer to the dilemma until my resourceful O'Badiah whispered in my ear. He recalled my triumph at the Harlot's Ball last year, where I had won top honors as Drag Queen of Babylonia. King Tiglath, he reminded me, had ordered "any and all daughters" of Azubah and Jeroboam to be brought before him. Posing as a third princess, I could obey the Queen's command and be on hand to wangle the best deal possible for Princess Deborah. With the Queen's assent, we bowed out of the royal presence and hightailed it to our room at one of Nineveh's well appointed inns.

O'Badiah wasted no time assembling tools of the makeover trade in our suite at the inn. I returned from the baths to find him arranging makeup, brushes, cosmetics and perfumes on a dressing table. He had also seen to it that the room was stashed with wigs on wig stands, a chest of fine jewelry, a rack of robes and tunics fit for a princess and a newly installed wall mirror of highly polished metal.

I was quick to put myself in his capable hands. "I'm ready for my makeover, O'Badiah. Turn me into a princess."

"A princess who will make King Tiglath swoon?" he asked playfully.

"Don't overdo it, darling," I replied. "To be permitted in the throne room, I just need to pass for one of the Queen's daughters. An ugly daughter will suffice."

"Remember," said O'Badiah, "the female face and shape and dress I can give you. But the essence of Woman: That's up to you."

I understood: "Ahh, you mean movement, mannerisms, attitude."

"I mean a dog can be disguised as a cat," he said. "But if the cat barks . . . and wags its tail . . ."

"Don't worry," I replied. "I won't bark. But I will wag my tail."

It had taken a virtual army of cosmeticians and stylists to transform Abigail #42 into a convincing princess. O'Badiah was aiming for a similar transformation of yours truly, but he had far less to work with.

As he shaded my neck to make it appear more slender, he commented, "I feel sorry for those who must live their lives in only one gender."

"A very limited existence," I agreed. "Who couldn't benefit from an occasional change of gender?"

He carefully shaped a comely wig with blonde curls around my head and stepped back to admire his handiwork. "You are a work of art, my sweet."

It was now time to squeeze me into a tortuous bone corset. "Inhale, m'lady, inhale," he commanded and pulled the corset laces tight with all his considerable might: "Fashion demands a tiny female waist. And when the corset pinches, repeat after me, 'beauty must suffer.'"

Without asking my opinion, O'Badiah selected a regal red robe off the rack and guided me into it. One look in the mirror verified his choice. "Princesses are born for red!" he exulted.

O'Badiah had previously selected the jewels he thought worthy of a newly manufactured princess. He ceremoniously bedecked me with rings, bracelets, earrings and necklaces. and crowned me with a magnificent tiara.

The final addition to my splendiferous regalia was a boa, which he tentatively draped over my shoulders before deciding in its favor.

Circling to appraise me from every angle, O'Badiah rendered his verdict: "You are ravishing, my darling. No other word for it."

When I examined my new self critically in the mirror, I saw his point. "Come and get it, Tiggy, baby," I said, swiveling my hips.

"By all means," answered O'Badiah, "Come and get her, Tiggy,the Piggy!"

We began to laugh helplessly, and I might have continued to the point of tears but for concern about smearing my makeup.

24

ABIGAIL #42

I saw very little of Jonah after we joined the caravan to Nineveh. The last time I laid eyes on him, he was hang-dogging behind Deborah's camel, content with his degrading assignment as last footman in the pecking order. Deborah was engaged to the most powerful monarch in the Known World and gave Jonah next to no encouragement, yet he refused to accept the impossibility of eventually winning her love. I could relate to that: Jonah despised me, and rightly so, for leading him on a wild goose chase that nearly cost him his life, yet I refused to accept the impossibility of eventually winning his affection.

When we arrived in Nineveh, Philo took me under his wing and arranged a suite adjacent to his in one of the city's finest inns. He and O'Badiah kept a watchful eye, making sure I was never alone on the thoroughfares of the wicked city. Shortly Philo brought surprising news: My princess status had been reinstated, and I would be presented to King Tiglath as a sister of Princess Deborah. He offered no further explanation. But it was obvious that I had become a token on a political board game—with King Tiglath on one side, Queen Azubah and Philo on the other. The best I could hope for was to be one of the tokens left standing at game's end.

25

PHILO

At the designated hour our royal foursome arrived promptly for our appointment in the throne room of King Tiglath of Assyria. Since only royalty were permitted, I had honored Queen Azubah's command to be present by posing as her third daughter. The King would be introduced to one authentic princess of Samaria and two pretenders—Princess Abigail and Princess Philomena (that was me). As to what would ensue after the introduction of three princesses to the great sovereign, I had nary a clue. And if Queen Azubah had a plan, she didn't confide it to me.

All I knew was that my masquerade as Princess Philomena would have to be the performance of my life. If King Tiglath found me out, he would have my head. And so would my Queen if I failed her. So in fact this was to be a performance *for* my life.

Two burly palace guards with javelins at the ready ushered us into the throne room. We were immediately struck by its awesome dimensions and over-sized furnishings. Enormous ceramic jugs, which the Assyrians call "amphora," flanked the entrance. On the facing wall was a gigantic map of inlaid silver titled, "The Known World"—with Greater Assyria at its dominant center. All surrounding countries on the map, including Samaria, were rendered smaller and punier by comparison.

One of the heralds unrolled a scroll and instructed us: "All kneel before the Supreme Ruler of Assyria, greater than Egypt, greater than Babylon and becoming greater every day."

We knelt before an imposing marble stairway, which led up to a shimmering golden throne too bright to behold with open eyes. The image of the exalted figure on the throne was blurred by the squint-inducing glitter of gold.

The herald continued to address the distant monarch at the top of the palatial staircase: "Humbly beseeching His Royal Highness now come Queen Azubah of Samaria and her trio of princesses."

"You may rise," said a deep authoritative voice from on high. "You may gaze upon me."

"I'm blinded, Your Greatness," said Queen Azubah. "Your throne is brighter than the sun."

"And getting brighter every day," replied the booming voice, echoing off the marble walls. "State your business."

"Business of state," Azubah answered. "To conclude a matrimonial alliance between Assyria and Samaria, I offer you a choice of one of my three daughters—priceless princesses all."

"We are discussing a marriage of convenience," said the King. "So which of your princesses will be most convenient for me?"

"If I may presume to advise you, Your Majesty," the Queen replied. "As their mother I am well positioned to assess their comparative virtues."

"By all means, Queen Mother." agreed King Tiglath. "Please proceed."

Queen Azubah had clearly seized the moment and taken full charge of our audience with the great King of Assyria. Her experience hen-pecking King Jeroboam had honed her talent for managing male royalty. I had no idea where she was headed with her presentation, but she was hell-bent on controlling the proceedings.

"I humbly suggest," said Azubah to the ascendant King, "that the question you must answer today, is which one of these lovely ladies has the right stuff to be your queen."

"Absolutely. Absolute monarch material is requisite," agreed Tiglath. "And the maiden's names?"

The Queen led the three of us to the foot of the stairway, where we dutifully beamed enticing smiles skyward through the forbidding golden haze. Each of us curtsied to the King as we were introduced. (O'Badiah had spent hours teaching me a proper, demure curtsy.)

"Princess Deborah, Princess Abigail, Princess Phill-o-meen-a," announced Queen Azubah.

It was a sore point with me when my name was pronounced with a short "i," so I was quick to voice my objection to the monarch looming above: "I prefer PHI-lo-meen-a, Your Majesty," I said.

"Oh, Phil-o-men-a, Shmil-o-me-na," the King kvetched. "To simplify matters I order the young ladies to be called Princesses A, B and C. Bring in the ribbons!"

Palace servants entered promptly with ribbons labeled "Princess A, "Princess B" and "Princess C," which they draped across Deborah as "A," Abigail as "B" and myself as "C."

Unperturbed, the Queen again took command: "Be forewarned, Your Highness. I will present the flaws of each Princess as well as her felicities."

"All the better," came the pronouncement from above.

"Princess A," proclaimed the herald as Deborah was led to center stage.

"Of all my daughters, Your Majesty," commenced Queen Azubah, "Deborah—the designated Princess A—is by far the most beautiful." This opening line pleased the aforesaid princess immensely. She turned to give King Tiglath a better view of her striking profile, which has often been compared with the Egyptian queen, Nefertiti. "However," Azubah continued, "this daughter of mine has certain predilections I feel obliged to report. For instance, she has a strong aversion to the word, 'obey,' be it in the traditional wedding vow or any other context. I have tried to suppress such feminist inclinations to no avail. In support of her ornery beliefs she has brought with her a manifesto stating her female rights and delineating strict terms of marriage acceptable to her. It will be posted on her bedroom door on your wedding night, and you will be expected to affix your signature in agreement before entering."

Princess Deborah was taken aback by her mother's fabrications. She was in tears as I heard her speak to the Queen under her breath: "Mother, you double-crossed me. This is not what we rehearsed."

"You will thank me one day, my darling," her mother replied.

26

ABIGAIL # 42

The morning I was presented to King Tiglath was full of surprises. I could not believe it when a third princess joined our entourage. The ruse was so unexpected that at first I didn't recognize the new princess as Philo in drag. His sheer temerity struck me as fraught with danger. I had been forewarned that candidates for Queen of Assyria must submit to a virginity test. I could pass, and I presumed Princess Deborah could pass. But Philo? What would become of us if we all were forced to submit to such a test?

The second surprise came when Queen Azubah introduced her real daughter. We had been designated Princess A, (Deborah). Princess B (me) and Princess C (Philo as Philomena). After announcing that Deborah was the most beautiful among us, which I thought was open to question, the Queen proceeded to portray her as a rabid feminist who would insist that King Tiglath sign a radical bill of female rights to gain entrance to her bedroom.

No love was lost for Princess Deborah on my part. But I was almost sorry for the arrogant snob as she left center stage in tears, visibly shaken and cursing her mother. My sympathies were cut short when the herald announced the presentation of "Princess B" to the king. It was my turn to show my "Princess Stuff" to the Supreme Ruler. Queen Azubah had decided I would demonstrate my dancing talent, which was considerable and had been a key to my success as a Royal Prophetess.

In rehearsal the dance I improvised had greatly pleased the Queen and Philo. Accompanied by a small combo—lyre, shepherd's horn and drum, I ended my dance with terpsichorean spins and a well executed split. My finale actually earned a few handclaps from King Tiglath on high.

"As you have witnessed, Princess B is an accomplished dancer," Queen Azubah told the King. "And she is herself pleasant enough to behold. But in fairness I must reveal she has one small idiosyncrasy. Although she held her water in this performance, she often feels free to squat on the dance floor and pee."

"Nobody's perfect," said King Tiglath. "Can she do 'The Continental?'"

I knew immediately what dance the King was referring to—a suggestive Assyrian two-step that had become a rage in the region, even in uptight Samaria. "I can, Your Highness," I told him.

"Yes, she can," seconded the Queen. "She does 'The Continental.' But she does it incontinently."

27

PRINCESS DEBORAH

I entered King Tiglath's throne room with high hopes. I had taken the word of my mom and Philo that presenting three princesses was a merely a tactic to help Samaria get the best possible deal in a matrimonial alliance. I was confident that my mother had given in to my ambition, and I would soon be crowned Queen of Assyria.

I was in for a rude awakening. Once in the throne room Mumsy proceeded to undermine my cause, describing me as a feminist vixen who would soon rob the King of his authority, his self respect and his balls. Then she trashed Abigail for lack of bladder control. It seemed that my mother, the Queen, wished to place all her princesses in the worst possible light.

Seeing that Abigail and myself had been thoroughly denigrated, Philo began to panic. "What are you up to, my Queen?" I heard him mutter to Mother. "Surely you're not planning to recommend me."

With a wicked smile she retorted, "Could be!"

The herald escorted Philo as Princess Philomena to the forefront and announced: "Princess C, Your Majesty!"

Flustered and off balance, Philo's curtsy to the King was shaky at best.

But my mother could hardly contain her enthusiasm: "This royal rose, Your Supremeness, has been trained since infancy in the fine arts of being keenly queenly. She need not be taught to look down her nose, because that view is bred into her royal bones. She's a princess-perfect C, and the two of you will make a glorious Mister and Mrs. Majesty."

Philo was bewildered. "This is madness," he whispered to my mom. "Surely you can't be serious."

"I'm putting the game in your hands, Philo, she replied. "I want to see how you wriggle out of this one!"

Then Mother led me front and center for a final curtsy to the King and requested a drum roll from the drummer.

"Princess A," she announced, "is second runner-up. Better luck next time," she told me and dismissed me with a blown kiss.

Then she brought Abigail forward and asked for another drum roll: "Princess B is the proud first runner-up. In the event the new queen is unable to perform her duties . . ."

Mom's dramatic presentation was abruptly interrupted by King Tiglath: "You've sold me, Queen Azubah. I'll take the lot."

"I beg your pardon," said my mother.

"My decision is I will marry all three," the King affirmed.

Mumsy was nonplussed: "All three? But surely Your Majesty . . ."

"My decision is final," snapped the King.

Further entreaties were met with silence. The herald then announced, "All present are excused. The King has departed his throne."

"Oh, he is a piggy," I said to my mom, "to want all of us."

"If he does take the three of us to bed," said Philo, "he'll get more than he bargained for."

28

JONAH

Joel and I knew it was only a matter of time before we would be arrested for activities the authorities could not tolerate for long. Late one evening we were taken into custody and spent the night in a filthy pen we shared with assorted beggars, pickpockets and drunks. The next day we were brought before several Assyrian courts where arguments ensued about what crime we had committed. It was finally decided we would be charged with nay-saying, which could be adjudicated only by the King.

Brought in chains to the palace gates, we were turned over to a strapping giant of a man who was, he informed us, Royal Executioner. He patiently explained that nay-saying was a capital crime punishable by death when so ordered by the monarch. Though he claimed to be sympathetic to our cause, the executioner thought our chances were slim since nay-saying happened to be one of the King's pet peeves. Whistling as he wrote an order for our execution, our amiable captor said he would bring his axe with him in case he was called upon to expedite our beheadings.

We were escorted into King Tiglath's throne room with heavy hearts. Dragging his great axe behind him, the executioner held up his official order and addressed the king, whom he presumed sat aloft in the golden haze above: "I, Thor, request that His Majesty initial this Order of Execution of these pests. They are predicting the destruction of Nineveh and must be condemned as nay-sayers."

I appealed to the King: "Nineveh may not necessarily be destroyed. It can be saved, Your Highness."

"If Nineveh will repent," said Joel.

Are you not nay-sayers?" the executioner demanded to know.

86

"Nay," said Joel, and I immediately corrected him: "He meant to say, 'No.'"

I had realized by this time that there was nobody up yonder on the distant throne. "I think the King's on a break," I said to Thor.

"We'll wait," he replied and began to sharpen his axe.

29

PHILO

When King Tiglath announced he would marry all three princesses, our Samaritan royal retinue was thrown for a loop. No sooner had the King left his throne than palace guards led us into a reception hall, where we were directed to wait for the King. With every exit blocked by armed soldiers, we were clearly being held prisoners. A bleak situation became even bleaker when Jonah and Joel were led into the hall in chains by a monster of a man wearing an executioner's mask and dragging an enormous axe. Despite the Phoenician adage that "misery loves company," the sight of the shackled scribes, forlorn in sackcloth and ashes, only compounded our misery.

The melancholy was suddenly interrupted by a boy in full battle dress, with helmet, armor, sword, bow and a quiver of arrows. The youngster appeared to be playing at war. Seizing a javelin from one of the soldiers, he pretended to lead a military attack. "Storm the ramparts. Javelins, ho!" he cried and sent the javelin flying over our heads, narrowly missing Queen Azubah.

"You should be more careful with your toys, sonny," said the Queen. "You could put someone's eye out."

"Do your mother and father work at the palace?" I asked the boy.

"No," he replied. "But I work here."

"My gracious!" said the Queen. "Don't you people have child-labor laws?"

"Sure," the boy answered. "But I'm exempt. Because, I'm like . . . the King."

We were stunned by the youngster's claim. "But we just had an audience with the King," said Azubah. "We heard his deep and mature voice."

The boy gleefully threw off his helmet, leaped to the rim of an amphora and thrust his head inside the huge vase. "You may rise," echoed a booming voice. "You may gaze upon me." Raising his head from the amphora, he giggled impishly, catapulted himself backwards out of the amphora and landed nimbly on his feet. "That's a trick I love to play on strangers, he said. "Make no mistake," he added. "I am Tiglath, King of Assyria."

We attempted to pay our respects, but before we could kneel Tiglath ordered us up. "Nix to the kneeling," he said and then seemed to notice Jonah and Joel for the first time. "Who are these bums?" he asked.

"They are our countrymen, Your Majesty," I explained, "accused of nay-saying."

"We pray you will spare them," offered Abigail.

Young Tiglath had hardly considered Abigail's plea before he proclaimed, "Off with their heads!"

The executioner took the little king at his word, struggling to lift the great axe. Tiglath intervened and picked it up with ease. "Weakling!" he said, "I'll do it myself." Twirling the axe above him, he approached Jonah and Joel, who prepared for imminent demise. "Just kidding!" he said. He threw the axe to the executioner, who caught it and fell to the floor under its weight. "As a kid I'm allowed to kid," he told us, "Like when I said I'd marry all three of you. I can't even bear the thought of one wife. I'm a normal twelve year-old boy. I hate girls."

"We are surprised by your youth," said Queen Azubah. "We were expecting . . ."

"An old fart?" asked King Tiglath.

"We heard you were an old but fearsome warrior, my Lord," I said.

"Old, no," replied the King, "Fearsome, yes." Pulling his sword from its sheath, he handled it with practiced skill as he thrust and parried his way around the reception hall. His impressive exhibition of swordsmanship was followed by a demonstration of his prowess in archery. He took an arrow from his quiver and nonchalantly aimed it at Joel's doomsday sign on the opposite side of the great reception hall. The arrow struck Joel's placard precisely where needed to make a perfect period after "REPENT OR DIE."

"I strive to be the equal of the best in my army with sword, bow and javelin," boasted the young King. "When I engage the enemy, it'll be like 'Where the Hell did that little bastard come from?'"

"Doubtless you will prove yourself a fine soldier." I ventured. "But how is it we've been hearing for years about the fierce and mighty King Tiglath?"

"Now the truth can be told," he answered. "When my parents died and I became King, I was a helpless infant. But the governing regents spread rumors that Assyria was now ruled by a fierce old warmonger."

Queen Azubah appreciated royal chicanery when she heard of it. "What a brilliant disinformation campaign!" she marveled. "And were the regents responsible for your nickname?"

King Tiglath chuckled. "Not at all," he said. "I earned the nickname, 'Tiggy, the Piggy,' because I was the fattest baby under the sun." Then with willful adolescent petulance, he complained, "And now those damn sissy regents won't let me go to war in the north without securing my southern flank."

"Yes, of course," said Queen Azubah with renewed confidence. "A matrimonial alliance with Samaria will assure our neutrality."

"My army is ready to march, and those cowardly regents are like, 'Restrain yourself, Tiggy, you mustn't risk a war on two fronts!' Just to keep those namby-pambies happy, I have to . . ." He paused and held his nose to show his distaste: ". . . get married." The little king then strode among us, the three princesses, and pointed his sword at Princess Deborah. "She will be my Queen," he announced.

"I am truly honored to be your selection," responded Princess Deborah with a cold eye to her mother, which pointedly conveyed, "No thanks to you."

"You can be the bitchy big sister I never had," Tiglath told her. "And feisty enough to keep the regents in line while I'm at war."

"But why must you go to war?" Queen Azubah asked.

"It's like . . . traditional in this region," replied the King. "And if I'm going to conquer the world, I have to start young."

"For me I'm afraid war is beyond understanding," said Azubah.

"How can women understand war?" asked Tiglath, directing his question to Jonah and Joel, "What do they know of the siege, the assault, the scaling of the barricades through a fusillade of flaming arrows? It's exhilarating work!"

With a wary eye to the executioner sharpening his axe, Jonah tended to agree with the King. "And healthy too," he said, "You're fighting out in the fresh air."

"With plenty of room for advancement," Joel asserted, "Your bosses keep getting killed."

Tigtlath pointed his sword at a map on the wall, a duplicate of the Known World map we had seen in the throne room. "First I will attack Phrygia, Lygia and Tygia," he promised. "Then Tubal, Rubal and Ubal. Next comes Thrace, followed by Phlace and Mace."

"The kid sure has a long shit list," Joel whispered to me.

"He's some kind of prodigy," said Jonah. "Like one of those little geniuses who can pick up a lyre for the first time and play beautiful music."

"Yes," I agreed, "but this genius makes war instead of music."

"I will call a meeting with those yellow-bellied regents at once," announced King Tiglath. "Now that I've secured Assyria's southern flank, I can at long last go to off to war!"

Before leaving the reception hall the boy-king issued orders to his palace guards. Queen Azubah and her princesses, me included, were graciously escorted to comfortable quarters in the palace. But my last glimpse of Jonah and Joel was most disconcerting. They were being roughly pummeled toward a barred gate bearing the word, "hovva," Assyrian for "dungeon."

30

JONAH

I had heard about palace dungeons but had not been unfortunate enough to be thrown into one until the arrogant child-king incarcerated Joel and me in the oubliette under his palace. We were there, according to our tormentors' official directives, "Pending disposition by the King,"

The boy-king's whims were worrisome enough. But we were even more concerned about Yahweh's timetable. "How are we going to get out of here before Yahweh lowers the boom on Nineveh?" Joel asked.

"Leave it to Yahweh," I said. "He'll think of something."

At that very moment, Princess Deborah and Abigail unlocked and entered our dungeon cell. "We've come to save you," said Abigail.

"That was fast," I remarked to the Almighty above. Then turning to Deborah I said, "You've come to rescue me, haven't you, my love?"

"As Queen-Designate, I have a duty to visit all condemned men," was her icy reply. And referring to Joel, she added, "especially your friend here—the incredible hunk."

"We bring good news," said Abigail. "The King may grant you a pardon."

"Philo is making it a clause in the pre-nuptial," announced Princess Deborah. "How lucky can a girl get?" she mused as she stroked Joel's face. "Of all the walls of all the dungeons under all the palaces in the world—you're chained to mine."

"You're smearing my ashes," objected Joel.

The Princess picked up his ankle chain. "You're even sexier on a leash," she told him.

I didn't know what offended me more—the engagement of Deborah to the young King Tiglath or her blatant overtures to my best friend.

"Is it official now," I asked the Princess, "that you're actually going to marry a twelve-year-old?"

"So my husband will be an adolescent," she replied. "Aren't they all?"

I countered with: "And when do you take this child to be your . . . ."

The Princess interrupted: "In exactly nine days."

"What a coincidence! That's the same day Nineveh is going to blow," I was pleased to tell her. "Yahweh will provide the fireworks for your wedding gala."

"We won't even be in Nineveh," she said. "I want a country wedding. So I ordered the brat-king to get us hitched at our palace in Tarshish."

"You seem to have made all the necessary arrangements," I replied, not even trying to hide my resentment.

"Yes, except for one urgent matter," she said. "I mean the loss of my friggin' virginity for crying out loud."

Turning her back on me, she brazenly embraced Joel, who tried to fend her off with his doomsday sign. "The King is just a little boy-beau, honey, she purred. "So the Queen is appointing you her concu-beau." Showing off her conquest to Abigail, she asked, "Isn't he the handsomest?"

"Abigail wouldn't know," said Joel. "She only has eyes for Jonah."

"Yes," Abigail admitted. "And Jonah loves Debby, who's hot for Joel, who I have been told yearns for me."

"I do," said Joel. "The four of us are some kind of dysfunctional daisy chain."

"I bet my concu-beau is functional," said Princess Deborah, exploring Joel's sackcloth with her forefinger and looking at me to see how much jealous rage she was arousing.

Abigail pulled a ring of keys from her gown and suggested, "I think it's time to get these guys out of their shackles."

"Hold it!" said Princess Deborah. "First let's see if they're ready to make a commitment."

31

JOEL

Brought before the kid-king Tiglath, Jonah and I knew he was anxious to dispense with our case in the interest of his impending alliance with Samaria. To our advantage, we were an impediment that he had to deal with so he could go off to war. But we held little hope that he would be moved by our dire message from a foreign god.

Unrolling a scroll enumerating our crimes, he said, "It's hard to believe my people do all these wicked things you report."

"King Tiglath," Jonah replied. "your Assyrian subjects routinely commit adultery, sodomy, incest, bestiality . . ."

"Bestiality? What's that?" asked the king.

"Sex with animals," I answered. "namely sheep, goats, oxen, ostriches."

"An ostrich is a bird, not an animal," said Tiglath.

"You are correct, Your Majesty," Jonah replied. "But you can't get off on a technicality. Nineveh will be destroyed in seven days."

The cocky little king was not intimidated. "Says who?" he asked.

"Yahweh," Jonah replied.

"That's our Hebrew god," I said.

"Our goddess Assura is the Great Protector of Assyria," Tiglath asserted.

"With all due respect, Your Highness," Jonah told him, "a one-on-one between Yahweh and Assura would be no contest."

Pointing to our doomsday signs, Tiglath said, "Suppose I believed this nonsense. Is there anything I could do about it? If not, what's the point?"

Until this moment not a single soul in Nineveh had shown a shred of belief in our apocalyptic message. We were surprised to find that the underage head of a great nation seemed now to be considering it. "It is written," said Jonah, "that what you can do about it is repent and atone."

"To repent, we just say we're sorry, right?" replied King Tiglath.

"Right," we answered in unison.

"That's easy enough," was the king's response. "But how do we atone?"

Jonah was eager to instruct the young king: "First, you must cast off prideful raiment and wear sackcloth and ashes as we do."

"So as an exercise in humility, I don sackcloth and ashes," said the King. "Then what?"

"Second," I told him, "you must forswear jewelry and perfume."

"Jewelry and perfume, yuck! That's no problem." replied Tiglath.

It was beyond belief that the King of Assyria seemed to be pondering Yahweh's terms.

"Yahweh's third and final requirement," said Jonah, "is that you make a pilgrimage of atonement, traveling with other contrite Assyrians to Yahweh's temple in New Samaria."

"All in sackcloth and ashes?" asked Tiglath, and when we assented, he said, "Cool! And how many Assyrians wearing sackcloth and ashes would it take to change Yahweh's mind? Might ten thousand penitent souls do the trick?"

"I can't speak for Yahweh," I replied. "But we have an expression: It couldn't hurt."

"Well, our goddess, Assura, has been goofing off lately," said the King. "So why not try your god, Yahweh, for a change? I will organize an expedition—I mean, a pilgrimage—of ten thousand penitents. We will march—I mean we will journey—to New Samaria in sackcloth and ashes. That should make Yahweh chill out about Nineveh."

"But Your Majesty," said Jonah, "what about your wedding to the Princess?"

"I can't get married in sackcloth and ashes," Tiglath replied. "So the wedding's off." He headed for the exit but before leaving he added, almost as an after thought, "Meanwhile, you're like . . . pardoned."

"We're free!" I shouted.

"Yes," said Jonah. "I'm free to pursue my beautiful Princess again."

"Yes," I agreed. "And I'm free to catch Abigail on the rebound."

32

KING TIGLATH

Fifty years later, looking back on my first military campaign as a naïve, impetuous twelve year-old, I can only say that the stars must have been aligned in my favor. An experienced general now, I have conquered most of the civilized countries in the Known World, all of whom pay homage (and taxes) to Greater Assyria. But my first conquest was both the boldest and riskiest venture of my career. I actually took the word of a couple of religious fanatics that the gates of their capital would open to any and all Assyrians who arrived dressed in sackcloth and ashes seeking atonement from their Hebrew god, Yah-woo, Yah-woe, Yah-something-or-other. Would a seasoned military strategist take a gamble on such a premise? Certainly not. But I was a boy and had reached the age where I knew better than my elders.

Previously I had been hondling with the Hebrews about guaranteeing peace on our southern flank by marrying one of their princesses, a horrific prospect at the age of twelve. Instead I sent the princesses packing, along with their overbearing mother, and requisitioned enough sackcloth to provide a new wardrobe for my army. Or should I say, "war-robe?"

I knew for certain that our governing regents would never approve the rash adventure I was planning. So I informed them I was taking the army on maneuvers again. I sealed the deal by promising we would mop up the marauding bandits who were harassing our southern caravan routes.

The operation against Samaria went as smoothly as sand flows through an hourglass. Ten thousand strong, in sackcloth and ashes, we knelt abjectly before the fortress walls of New Samaria. The Hebrew priests ordered the gates opened, and we entered piously, pretending to seek atonement. Beneath our sackcloth, we had strapped our swords, bows and javelins. Samaria's army never suspected it, but we were dressed to kill.

The ensuing battle proved how important is the element of surprise in warfare. In a matter of hours we subdued a Samarian army more than double the size of our own. The ashes on our Assyrian faces gave us an unexpected advantage: Many of the Samaritan soldiers mistook us for the awesome warriors from Africa and ran away in terror. Before nightfall, flags of surrender appeared on the fortress Parapets. New Samaria was ours!

33

PHILO

It was a masterpiece of military deception! The boy-king Tiglath took New Samaria and the rest of our Kingdom soon thereafter. With this notch in his belt, the young military genius needed only ten more years to conquer the entire Known World, at least those parts worth conquering. He had become Master Of The Universe at a mere twenty-two.

Bereft of their nationhood, the Hebrew people turned from the secular to the spiritual. It was now clear that reform had been Yahweh's will and purpose all along, acting through his prophet, Jonah. He and Joel were pronounced Major Prophets, their wisdom sought throughout the Kingdom.

After becoming a province of Assyria, Samaria had no further use for its monarchs. King Jeroboam and Queen Azubah were swiftly deposed. The conquerors enforced the laws of the land but entrusted moral imperatives to the high priests, who were now empowered to take a more fundamental, scripture-driven approach to religion. Attendance at temple services, for instance, was no longer voluntary. Even my condensed bible stories were banned by the high priests until government officials, noticing a loss of revenue, reinstated them.

Jonah and Joel were bestowed a comfortable residence, built by a grateful people for their illustrious prophets. When the government decided to provide a servant couple as cook and butler, the prophets were kind enough to hire the former king and queen, previous grievances notwithstanding.

I dine frequently at the home of the prophets. Over the years and between wars, King Tiglath has occasionally found time to join us for brunch. The former queen, now a cook, continues to browbeat the former king, now a butler, even in their reduced circumstances.

"Wine vessel on the left, Jeroboam," she will instruct. "And stop ogling that chambermaid."

Princess Deborah and Abigail Number #42 turned out to be model wives of prophets. "Surely Jonah married Princess Deborah," you may be thinking, Considering the travails of Jonah in pursuit of the Princess, their union might appear to have been the will of God. But the will of God, I contend, doesn't hold a candle to the will of Woman. In the end Abigail #42 snagged Jonah and Deborah caught Joel. The women got their men, which according to my experience, is pretty much old news.

While far from benevolent, the Assyrian rule proved to be no more arbitrary or tyrannical than that of the monarchy. In fact with respect to eunuchs, their administration has been gratifyingly lenient. Shortly after taking control, the new government repealed the law forbidding a eunuch to have a lover. O'Badiah and myself immediately went public with our affection.

As head of the Royal Library, I continued to turn a profit for the state until my vision became clouded a few years ago. O'Badiah and I are both pensioners now. We've been openly living together since 999 B.C.

999 B.C.! A year in which it was my special privilege to be alive and at the center of events.

APPENDIX

SCENES & SONGS FROM THE MUSICAL, *999 B.C.*

ACT I

1. The archives of the Royal Library of New Samaria (949 B.C.)
   The Scroll Copycenter / The Bureau Of Divine Wisdom (999 B.C.)
   999 B.C .... Old Philo & Company
2. On a riverbank
   Song Of Solomon .... Jonah & Princess Deborah
   Ouch! .... Jonah
3. The Scroll Copycenter / The Bureau Of Divine Wisdom
   The Scribblers' Song .... Philo, Jonah & Joel
   On The Other Hand .... Abigail
4. Princess Deborah's dressing chamber / The Royal Armory
5. The Royal Class Lounge of the Caravan Terminal
6. Outside the Royal Class Lounge
   Oasis On The Joppa Trail .... Queen Azubah, Jonah & Joel
7. A mead joint in New Samaria
   Nineveh .... Philo, King Jeroboam & O'Badiah
   The Eunuch Blues .... O'Badiah
8. The stern deck of King Tiglath's flagship
   A *Captain's Prayer* .... Captain Hiram & Company

ACT II

MUSIC BIBLIOGRAPHY
(Act I)

Scene 1
999 B.C.
To the tune of *Cute*—Music by Neal Hefti
Copyright 1958 Encino Music
Instrumental by Count Basie on Fairmont Records (1958)

Scene 2
Song Of Solomon
To the tune of *Lady Bird*—Music by Tadd Dameron
Copyright 1949 Consolidated Music Publishers, Inc.
Instrumental by Tadd Dameron and his Band (1949, Air-Check Series

Ouch!
To the tune of *Li'l Darlin'*—Music by Neal Hefti
Copyright 1958 Warner Brothers Music Corp.
Instrumental by Count Basie on Roulette Records (1958)

Scene 3
The Stumblers'Song
To the tune of *Stompin' Down Broadway*—Music by Ernest Wilkins
Copyright Embassy Music Corp.

On The Other
To the tune of *The*
Copyright 1948 Co. *Come*—Music by Dizzy Gillespie
Instrumental by Dizz ed Music Publishers, Inc.

Scene 6

Oasis On The Joppa Trail
To the tune of *Palm Garden*—Music by Thomas (Fats) Waller

Scene 7
Nineveh
To the tune of *9:20 Special*—Music by Earl Warren
Instrumental by Count Basie on Okeh Records

The Eunuch Blues
To the tune of *Kickin' The Blues*—Music by Ernest Wilkens
Copyright 1959 Embassy Music Corp.

Scene 8
A Captain's Prayer
To the tune of *Saint James Infirmary Blues* (Traditional folk song)
Instrumental by Artie Shaw on RCA Records (1943)

MUSIC BIBLIOGRAPHY
(Act II)

Scene 9
Why Don't We Pretend To Get Romantic?
To the tune of *Robbin's Nest*—Music by Sir Charles Thompson and "Illinois" Jacquet
Copyright 1947 Atlantic Music Corp.
Instrumental by "Illinois" Jacquet & his orchestra (1947), Apollo Records

Scene 12
Gender
To the tune of *Ridin'*—Music by Willie "The Lion" Smith and Jack Edwards
Copyright 1976 Consolidated Music Corporation

Scene 13
That Right Princess Stuff
To the tune of *Zaggin' With Zig*—Music by E. Bernardi
Instrumental by Benny Goodman and his orchestra

Why ***Man Goes Off To War***
To the t...
& Julian ...f *Tuxedo Junction*—Music by Erskine Hawkins, William Johnson
Instrumenta...
...rskine Hawkins and his band (1946), Bluebird Records

Scene 14
Do Unto Me
To the tune of *Yardb...
Instrumental by Char... —Music by Charlie Parker...

Scene 15
Sackcloth and Ashes
To the tune of *Skyliner*—Music by Charlie Barnet
Instrumental by Charlie Barnet and his orchestra (1944), Decca Record